Speechless

Speechless

JENNIFER MOOK-SANG

Scholastic Canada Ltd.
Toronto New York London Auckland Sydney
Mexico City New Delhi Hong Kong Buenos Aires

Scholastic Canada Ltd.
604 King Street West, Toronto, Ontario M5V 1E1, Canada

Scholastic Inc.
557 Broadway, New York, NY 10012, USA

Scholastic Australia Pty Limited
PO Box 579, Gosford, NSW 2250, Australia

Scholastic New Zealand Limited
Private Bag 94407, Botany, Manukau 2163, New Zealand

Scholastic Children's Books
Euston House, 24 Eversholt Street, London NW1 1DB, UK

www.scholastic.ca

Library and Archives Canada Cataloguing in Publication
Mook-Sang, Jennifer, author
Speechless / Jennifer Mook-Sang.
Issued in print and electronic formats.
ISBN 978-1-4431-4267-0 (pbk.).—ISBN 978-1-4431-4268-7 (html).—
ISBN 978-1-4431-4269-4 (Apple edition)
I. Title.
PS8626.O59264S64 2015   jC813'.6   C2015-901176-0
                                          C2015-901177-9

Cover image by Michela Sabine Fierro.

6 5 4 3   Printed in Canada 139   16 17 18 19 20

To Matt and Ben
— my inspiration —
For the Surprises
And the Laughter

1

The door of the school library burst open and Parker blasted in. "Hey, Jelly, you have *got* to come and see this!"

Parker's a good head taller than me and built like an SUV. When he pulls your arm, resisting could cause permanent damage. I let myself be dragged into the hallway as Ms Longo, the librarian, put her finger to her lips and said, "Shhh," behind us.

There was a huge crowd of kids jostling outside the main office. They were elbowing each other and saying, "Wow! Cool!" and "Ex-cellent!"

I removed Parker's meaty fingers and rubbed my arm. What was everyone looking at?

The big sign on the wall proclaimed: *Sherwood Forest Public School Annual Speech Competition.*

Oh, big deal. Every year, the students in grades three to six have to give a speech. And every year, I've mumbled mine as fast as I could and got it over with.

"So . . . ?" I turned to Parker.

"You should go for it this year," he said.

"You're kidding me, right? Why would anyone go through that torture just to win some lame medal?"

"Because," he said, "you've always wanted one of *those,* Jelly." Parker pointed at the display case beside the sign.

I caught my breath.

On the glass shelf gleamed a brand-new tablet computer. I blinked. With accessories. There was even a Bluetooth keyboard and a fancy drawing stylus and — this was unbelievable — a gaming controller.

My mouth fell open.

"*That's* this year's prize!" said Parker.

No wonder everyone was so excited.

My parents wouldn't even let me watch more than an hour of TV a day, and our computer was only for homework. Of course, I didn't own a single video game.

I gazed longingly at the glossy black device with its sleek case that folded into a stand. I thought about having my very own tablet, in my own room, and the games I could play on it — Z-World Tectonic, Journey to Outer Zed and, best of all, Battle MegaZed.

Too bad it was a *speech* contest.

Ahead of us, a girl said, "Oh! Look at that, Victoria."

"It doesn't matter what the prize is, Elsa," replied Victoria. "I compete for the challenge of it."

The sound of Victoria's voice always gave me the creeps. I rolled my eyes at Parker. But Victoria wasn't bragging. She was the student council president — the smartest girl in my class, and she never let anyone forget it. She was the first to answer questions, first to hand in her test before the end of the period and first to volunteer, even for stinky jobs like cleaning up the playground. Teachers loved her.

I felt Parker's fingers grip my arm again. "You could so win that thing."

Victoria's head swivelled around as I shook off his hand and joked, "Oh, sure, piece of cake."

Parker and I edged closer and inspected the display case until the bell signalled the end of recess. The mob of students vanished and Parker said, "Hey, Jelly, we're gonna be late."

He zoomed off before I could reply. I stared after him and thought how weird it felt that Parker wasn't in my class this year. When we were little, our moms said we stuck together like the insides of a sandwich. Since Parker

Brown's initials are P.B. and mine spell J.A.M. (for Joseph Alton Miles) . . . well, that's why everyone calls me Jelly.

I jogged to my locker, grabbed my binder and pencil case and ran to English.

T he classroom was buzzing. I slipped into my chair unnoticed while Ms Mitrovika clapped her hands and said, "Class, please . . ." The room gradually fell silent as she spoke. "I'm delighted you're so enthusiastic about the competition. You'll have two weeks to research, write and practise your speeches." She looked around expectantly. "Now, I know it's early, but has anyone thought about their topic?"

Guess whose hand shot up?

"Yes, Victoria?" said Ms Mitrovika.

"I'll be doing my presentation on . . ." she paused for dramatic effect, ". . . the conservation of biodiversity in South America."

Her best friends, Elsa and Becky, regarded her with open-mouthed awe. It figured. You could count on Victoria to choose a big, important subject, guaranteed to impress. A few other hands went up. There was the usual collection of mind-numbing ideas: my family's camping trip; why I love my cat; how to save electricity. My only serious competition would be Victoria.

What?

I'd be crazy to go up against her. But a picture of me playing Z-World Tectonic flashed in my mind. I smiled at the thought.

Ms Mitrovika looked in my direction. "Joe," she asked, "have you chosen a topic yet?"

My brain froze. I should have just said no. But I didn't. Instead, my mouth said, "Umm . . . I . . . I'd rather not share it at this time."

Ms Mitrovika raised an eyebrow. Everyone else said, "Oooooh," like they thought I was being mysterious. Except Victoria. She twisted around in her seat and whispered at me, "Hey, why don't you want to say your topic?" Her mouth turned down in a fake pout. "Is it that bad?"

Everyone around us stared and I wished I could think of something really clever to say. But, as usual, under pressure my mind had gone completely blank. Victoria turned back and put her hand up to answer the question the teacher had written on the board. I kept my eyes on the desk. I was afraid that people might actually *feel* the heat of my burning cheeks.

I didn't know what my speech was going to be about. But I knew one thing — I really wanted it to kick Victoria's speech's butt.

Later, as I rummaged through my locker for my lunch, Parker's familiar deep voice said, "Hey there, man of mystery."

I turned around to face him and his sister, Sam. They're twins but you'd never guess it. Sam's as tall as Parker and has the same sky-blue eyes but that's all they have in common. She has long, straight, dark brown hair — almost black. And she always looks tanned, as if she just got back from a Caribbean vacation. Parker has a head of fuzzy yellow hair and a face full of freckles.

"Hi, guys," I said. "Nice duds, P.B."

Under his lime-green hoodie, Parker's T-shirt declared, *I Embarrass My Family.*

"Yeah, I gotta keep up my dudely reputation."

Sam looked scornfully at him. "As if."

"So," said Parker, "we hear you've got some hot, top-secret idea for the speech contest."

"I do, I do."

"Well? Are you going to share it?" demanded Sam.

I couldn't admit I had no clue in front of Sam. "Sure . . ." I said. "But first tell me what you two are writing about."

Parker put his hand over his heart. "Mine will be about the thing that has changed my very being," he said. "I must tell the world about . . ." He leaned his forehead into his sister's shoulder. There was a catch in his voice. ". . . the demise of rock 'n' roll."

Sam laughed and shrugged him off. "That's so last century. I'm going to talk about why you should be more involved in your school community." She struck a pose. "And right now, I'm going to get involved with my school's hip hop club."

Sam did not look like she fit with the other girls in the hip hop club. She liked to wear long skirts, brightly coloured scarves and dangly earrings.

"No, no, no," said Parker. "What this school really needs is a rock 'n' roll club."

"Why don't you start one?" said Sam, "Maybe some of the older teachers would come." She grinned over her shoulder as she swished away.

Victoria strutted down the hall toward us, Elsa and Becky chattering around her. They stopped at one of the little clusters of girls at the lockers and Victoria said, "Don't forget — sleepover at my house on Friday."

They seemed excited. "Wouldn't miss it for anything," said one.

Victoria and her pals continued in our direction.

"Hey, girls," said Parker, smoothing back his wild hair.

Elsa smiled, but Victoria and Becky ignored him and stopped in front of me.

"I figured out why you didn't want to tell the class your idea, Jelly," said Victoria. "It's totally dumb, right?"

There was an awkward pause while I tried to think of a snappy comeback. Becky looked over at Victoria and laughed. Then Parker said, "Give it up, Victoria. Jelly's speech is gonna crush yours."

Her eyes flickered to him. Then she smiled coldly at me, and the three of them marched away.

Parker stared after the girls for a moment before he turned to me. "So, what *are* you doing for the contest?"

"It's spectacular," I said. "Stunning. Blow-your-mind amazing!"

He smiled at me. "You've got *no* idea?"

I shook my head.

Zilch. Nada. Nothing to the power of nothing.

4

I usually sat beside Parker on the school bus. But that afternoon his mom had picked him up for hockey practice so I ended up sitting with Spencer the brat.

I didn't mean to hurt him. But he kept whispering at me, "Jelly is a fart face," all the way home. Even though I told him to shut up. Even though I told him I'd tell the bus driver (he knew I'd never do that). Even though I told him I'd toss his hat off the bus (*I* knew I'd never do that). I took his hat and flapped it in the direction of the window, hoping that would make him stop. But as he reached to get it back the bus suddenly lurched around a corner and I lost my balance. My hand connected with his nose.

"Ow!" Spencer yelled. "What'd you do that for?"

He grabbed his hat and put it back on while he rubbed his nose. He started making fake sobbing noises.

I could tell he wasn't really hurt because in between every pretend sob, he giggled. I was about to apologize when a voice piped up behind us, "Excuse me, bus driver, ma'am, there's a problem back here." Victoria made her way to the front of the bus and talked to the driver while pointing at me and Spencer.

Usually Victoria paid us absolutely no attention. And last year's bus driver would have just yelled at us to stop being so noisy. But this new driver pulled over, stopped the bus and came down the aisle. "Did this boy hit you?" she asked Spencer.

He shrugged.

"Don't be scared," she said. "Just tell the truth."

Spencer nodded.

I started to explain, but the bus driver shook a finger at me and wrote down both our names. She said to me, "Next time, pick on someone your own size." Then she moved me to the front of the bus beside her.

I heard Victoria say loudly, "Some people think they can get away with anything."

I looked back at Spencer. He just grinned and stuck out his tongue at me. Brat.

* * * * *

The next day, I found myself in the principal's office. Mrs. Muddgrove called me a bully; then she called my mom at work. Mom knew all about Spencer. Later, she told me he probably deserved it but I should find a more mature way of dealing with him.

The principal thought it would be good for my character if I stayed in at recess and wrote a letter saying I was sorry for my evil ways. What she actually said was, "Joe, we expect sixth-graders to be good role models. You'll have to think about how your actions have affected another student and write a sincere letter of apology to Spencer."

I sat outside her office and wrote:

Dear Spencer,

I am sorry I hit you and made you cry. I apologize for hurting your nose and your feelings. I will try not to do it again.

<u>*Sincerely,*</u>

Joseph Alton Miles

I hoped he'd be steamed that I mentioned his crying and hurt feelings.

The principal didn't seem impressed by my letter and told me to stay in again the next day to draw a poster about bullying.

After school, Spencer came running over to Parker and

me in the bus line, waving my letter and singing, "Jelly says he's sorry."

He's a year younger than us but Spencer looks like he's in grade three. He's short and skinny and his mother buys him clothes two sizes up, for when he gets bigger. But he never grows into his baggy shirts and pants. He's also very annoying. We'd never let him hang out with us except he's outstanding at playing Rebel Ruckus.

Parker snatched the letter from Spencer and broke out laughing. "I can't believe you had to see the principal, Jelly," he said. "You *never* get in trouble."

It's true, I don't. But this year things feel different. Our school is named for the Sherwood Forest Park nearby. A long time ago, someone had the bright idea of making the story of Robin Hood the theme of the school. So the walls and lockers are painted Lincoln green, the colour worn by Robin and his Merry Men. And the motto of the school is helping others. That's all fine. But in gym, our teacher makes us do Little John jumping jacks and the Sherwood Forest shuffle. That does not feel cool. The washroom doors have silhouettes of people wearing tunics or dresses. They're so much alike that sometimes a person in a hurry could make an embarrassing mistake. Very not cool.

This stuff didn't bother me when I was little, but now that I'm in grade six it seems so babyish.

The rules feel especially ridiculous. Mr. Chan makes us line up to walk down the hall to computers. We might as well choose buddies and hold hands. At recess, we're not allowed to go inside the school without permission, and we can't go across the street to buy a pack of gum without a note from home. Walk, don't run. Quiet in the library. And Ms Mitrovika is constantly reminding us to wash our hands before lunch and to sneeze into our elbows.

This year, I can't catch a break. The one lunchtime I decided to toss my stuff at the trash can instead of going all the way across the room to drop it in, Mrs. Muddgrove happened to be walking by. I got a good telling-off right in front of everyone. Victoria laughed so hard she snorted.

I put my garbage in the can. Why does it matter how it gets there? I do my work. I don't bother anyone. They could cut me some slack on the unimportant things.

* * * * *

For my poster-drawing detention the next day, I made a comic strip of me dropping a colossal anvil on Spencer. The last panel showed him flattened like a pancake with a ring of stars and tweeting birds whizzing around his head. I put Xs over his eyes and made him a speech bubble that said, "I'm sorry I called you a fart face."

Then I threw it out and drew the principal pointing out of the picture and saying, "You *are* a fart face." It made me chuckle, but quietly, because I was in the library. I trashed that one too, but by then I felt better.

I finally drew a picture of a kid getting intimidated by a bigger kid while a bunch of others stood by and watched. I wrote a caption: *Speak Up, Speak Out!* I figured that could be a message to all the other kids on the bus who hadn't said a word to back me up when I tried to tell the bus driver that Spencer started it.

I had a lot of time on my hands during recess so I got some coloured pencils from Ms Longo and coloured in the poster. I made it 3-D, with shading and everything.

"This is really good, Joe," said Ms Longo when she looked at it. She's also our art teacher. "You should consider a career in art."

Painting landscapes and portraits? No thanks. But maybe someday I could design characters for a video game — *that* would be an excellent job.

"Thanks," I said, as the bell rang.

"How about I make a copy and enter it in the school board art contest?" she asked.

"Sure," I said. "But what's . . . ?"

Right then a whole crowd of kindergartners came charging in for storytime. She said, "I'll chat with you later, Joe," and turned around to greet them.

Everyone else started research for their speeches as I waited for inspiration. My classmates looked up how to care for your ferret; what keeps airplanes up; and the history of the Internet. Pretty soon I was sure all the good topics were gone. I took comfort in the fact that Parker wasn't working on his speech either.

"I know all there is to know about rock 'n' roll, dude," he declared. "I don't need to do research."

Toward the end of the first week, Victoria put up her hand and said, "I'm finished writing, Ms Mitrovika. Would you like me to help the others with their speeches?"

Ms Mitrovika said, "That's very generous of you. If anyone wants some assistance, let Victoria know."

Some people put their hands up and waved at her. She came over to Jeff at the desk beside me, pointed to his bibliography and said, "Six references? Is that all?" When he showed her what he'd written, she said, "Here, this is how I'd do it." She took his pencil and started crossing things out. "Take this part and put it there. Add a section on equipment and one on checking weather conditions. You need some more examples here. Where are your pictures?"

When she was finished, she turned to Jeff. "There! Perfect! Now all you need to do is figure out how camping's related to some important world event and work that in."

His shoulders slumped but he said, "Thanks, Victoria."

"You're welcome," she replied and turned to me. "I know you don't like to ask, Jelly," she said sweetly, "but I'd be happy to work on your speech with you. Maybe I could help you choose a *good* topic?"

My mouth opened but, as I expected, nothing came out. Victoria waited until I looked away, then stalked over to her next victim.

I told Parker about it later. "Why do they all pretend to like her? She's so mean."

"I don't think she's trying to be mean," he said. "And some of them *do* like her."

I had a strange thought. "P.B.! Do *you* like her?"

"No way!" he said, quickly. "Maybe people are afraid of her. Or jealous."

Jealous? *What?!* Parker must've caught a puck to the head at hockey and wobbled a few marbles loose. But he was right that some people were afraid of Victoria. I know I was.

* * * * *

On Friday afternoon, Parker didn't have a hockey practice or game. We jumped off the bus and headed to his house. Spencer trailed behind, making armpit noises. When we paid no attention, he started to poke us in the backs — hard. Finally, Parker turned around and said, "Spencer. If you don't stop that. Right. Now. You will never play video games with us again." The poking stopped.

We charged through Parker's front door and his mom stuck her head out of the kitchen. "Hello, boys. How was school today?"

"Fine, thanks, Mrs. Brown," we called as we raced down the stairs.

Parker's dad loves action movies, so he'd rigged up their basement with a big-screen TV and every kind of speaker. When we played video games, the surround sound plus the low, rumbly vibrations of the subwoofer made us feel like we were living inside a different world.

As Parker plugged in the controllers, Spencer said, "Can you believe that prize this year?"

"It's worth trying to win," I said. "If only I had a good topic."

"I already have my own computer and a video game system," said Parker. "I'm just aiming to pass."

Spencer said, "Speeches are boring. I'm going to do something to make people laugh."

"That's what *you* should do, Jelly," said Parker. "You're funny anyway — and that's just your face." I pretended to take a swing at him while he ducked and continued, "You could talk about your collection of weird questions grown-ups ask. Remember when your aunt wondered where watermelons come from if they don't have seeds?"

"And Jelly told her they adopt," Spencer said, grinning. "That's the kind of thing kids like."

"I can't tell jokes for a speech contest," I said.

"How about your favourite band or sports hero?" suggested Parker.

Didn't have one of either.

"C'mon, you guys," I said, "Victoria's won every speech contest since she was in grade three. What's a great topic?"

"If you're serious about winning," said Spencer, "it's gotta be about the biggest, most importantest issue there is — like world peace."

I sighed. "Guess I'll be making a speech about world peace."

"Groovy," said Parker. "Now let's play Ruckus."

In the midst of the usual on- and off-screen ruckus, Sam poked her head down the stairs and said, "Can't you guys hang out together without beating on each other?" We stopped our cushion fight and she said, "Mom made a snack."

We flew up the stairs and devoured Mrs. Brown's chocolate chip oatmeal cookies. "I love to see growing girls and boys eat," said Mrs. Brown. "Speaking of which, Sam, why don't you ask these fellows about Saturday?"

"Oh, yeah," said Sam. "P.B. and I were going to help out at the food bank, but he has to go out of town for hockey. We need someone to help sort cans of food."

"I can't," said Spencer. "I have to help my grandma move into her new condo."

Sam looked at me. "You can come, can't you, Jelly?"

I had no good excuse. I did try to think of one but I'm not good at thinking on my feet — or while sitting on my butt with my mouth full of cookies. So I nodded as vaguely as I could.

"Great," said Mrs. Brown. "We'll pick you up at eight tomorrow."

Eight? In the morning? Oh man! What had I gotten myself into?

6

When I left Parker's and went home, there was a spicy smell in our house. Mom had come home early from the speech clinic and made chickpea curry with steamed rice. Regrettably, she'd decided sautéed kale would be the perfect side dish. I helped set the table, and when Dad arrived, we sat down to dinner.

"The kids in my language therapy sessions were hilarious today," said Mom. "They made my week."

She passed a bowl of curry to me. "I asked one little guy what he was going to be for Halloween and he said, 'Me going to be a pumpkin.' So I corrected him, '*I'm* going to be a pumpkin.' He looked so surprised and then he said, 'Whoa, me too!'"

She scooped a generous portion of kale onto my plate and asked, "How was your week?"

I knew she didn't expect a real answer since she'd already heard about Spencer and the bus from the principal, but I thought I'd surprise her by telling her about the prize for the speech contest.

"That's nice," she said. "What are you going to talk about this year?"

I shrugged and put a tiny forkful of kale in my mouth.

Dad asked where the prize came from, and I told him someone's parents had donated it to the school. He frowned.

"I don't think that kind of thing is appropriate to give away at school," he said. "Everyone's already got TVs and computers and cellphones. Kids don't need another screen to stare at all day."

Then he turned to Mom. "Don't you agree, Gracie?"

Mom nodded her head in a yes-no kind of way.

"Well, what if I won it?" I burst out. "It wouldn't just be for playing games. I'd use it to do research and projects for school too."

Mom leaned back in her chair. "You're the expert, David," she said to Dad. "What do you think?"

Dad said, "Jelly, we have a perfectly good computer downstairs and lots of educational games. Why would you even want a tablet?"

I sighed. Having a dad who owned an electronics store didn't mean he let me try all the latest games. It was the opposite. He read magazines and newspaper articles that talked about how games turned kids into aggressive social outcasts. He said those stories scared him and he wasn't taking any chances with me. Give me a break!

"What else is new?" Mom asked.

I wasn't about to mention the extra detention I'd had but I did tell them about the food bank. Boy, did they get excited about that.

"Who else is going? What will you do? How will you get there?"

All I knew was, I was being picked up at the unreal hour of eight o'clock on a weekend morning.

"That's great!" said Dad.

"I'm so proud of you, Jelly bean," said Mom.

I'm sure she meant, *I'm shocked you're actually doing something that doesn't involve sitting in front of the computer all day.*

I thought of past conversations I'd had with my dad.

Dad: What do you want to do this summer?

Me: (shrug)

Dad: How about baseball or lacrosse or camping?

Me: Nah, I don't think so.

Dad: There's always soccer. You were a good little soccer player.

Good? I was as mediocre as all the other six-year-olds. Although, by the middle of the season, I'd gotten to know everyone on the team and I looked forward to the practices and pizza afterwards. The next summer, I said I could hardly wait to see Neil and Andrew and Coach Simon again. That's when Dad told me I'd probably be with a new coach and a different bunch of boys. "It'll be fun," he said. "You'll make new friends."

That was the end of my soccer career.

Once I'd suggested, "How about fencing, Dad?" I thought it'd be cool to wear a mask that made me look like a giant bee, and poke people with a sword. But Mom squelched that idea. She's a little more easygoing than Dad about technology but way more strict about sharp objects. So Dad spent his spare time in the summers teaching me how to do magic tricks and throw my voice. He'd put himself through college by being a children's entertainer. He can still juggle seven oranges at once. I can only do three.

After dinner, I loaded the dishwasher and wandered into the living room. Dad's old ventriloquist's dummy sat in one of the corner chairs. Dad liked to say they'd spent so much time together, Roger was like part of the family. I thought Roger's blond hair and round cheeks made him look a little bit like Parker.

"What's up, Roger?" I asked.

Roger stared straight ahead. Then he said, "Your butt in a sling, if you don't get writing that speech."

Roger was always honest with me, especially when no one was around to check if my lips were moving. And sometimes he had helpful advice.

"I don't know what to write about, Roger."

He said, "Write what you know."

Helpful.

I went to the basement and sat at the desk. I needed a topic that wouldn't make me look completely stupid in front of Victoria. A topic that would get me voted on to the finals.

I did what I always did when I had an important decision to make. I booted up the computer and went to work on a new game I was creating for my website.

It was bad enough that Saturday morning was cold and grey. Having to get up at the same time as I did for school really sucked. In the car, Sam and her mom argued about which station to play on the radio. We ended up having to listen to oldies music all the way to the food bank.

Sam's mom asked the usual exciting grown-up questions: How was school this year? Did I like my teachers? What were my extracurricular activities?

"Fine," I said. "They're okay." And, "I don't do any."

After that it was quiet, except for the hum of the car's heater and the disco music in the background. I noticed Sam's long, shiny hair and resisted the urge to pull her ponytail like I used to when we were younger. That would break the uncomfortable silence. But I didn't want her to think I was a little brat like Spencer.

I tried hard to think of something intelligent to say. I asked, "Does this place collect food for the homeless people around here?"

"Oh, no," said Sam. She swung around to see my face. "There are lots of people who need the food bank."

Sure. Of course. I nodded my head and tried to seem convinced. It wasn't hard. Sam could be very persuasive, and she was determined to save the world before she turned sixteen. I had to admit I kind of liked that about her.

But who would go to a food bank, anyway? Old men and old ladies, I guessed, dressed in dirty, shabby clothes — probably smelly.

"Um, how many people go to the food bank?" I asked.

"About two hundred families pick up groceries every month," said Mrs. Brown.

Two hundred? I thought. Wow. That sounded like a lot. And *families?* That meant children. There weren't any shabby-looking, smelly kids at my school. I wondered what it'd be like to not have enough food to eat. I shifted in my seat and watched the dark blur of trees and houses go by. This whole food bank trip was starting to feel sort of creepy.

Mrs. Brown pulled into the parking lot of a dingy strip plaza crammed with businesses like autobody shops, blind and shutter stores and places where people repaired things. The most interesting-looking one was called Motorcycle Mart. A bunch of shiny machines stood chained to a rail outside. A couple of big men with hairy faces and leather jackets leaned on the bikes, smoking. They stared at the car as we rolled past.

Mrs. Brown parked in front of a low, flat-roofed building with one small door and window. The sign over the door said *Food Share Partnership*. It was a tiny doorway. How could an entire warehouse of food fit in there?

I'd imagined shelves and shelves of food soaring to the ceiling of some giant storeroom. Instead, stepping into this building felt like going into a convenience store. It was warm and bright. The room had two long aisles and tall metal shelves piled with tins of vegetables and boxes of cereal. But there wasn't the huge variety of stuff that I saw when Mom or Dad made me go grocery shopping with them. Just lots and lots of a few different kinds of cans and boxes.

There were miniature shopping carts next to a big desk by the entrance. People were going up one aisle and down the other, reading labels and putting things in their carts. They were just like the people I'd seen at the supermarket.

Nothing smelled. It wasn't creepy either — until a deep voice boomed, sounding like the dull vibrations pulsing from a subwoofer.

"Hey, Rose. Hiya, Sam," said the voice. "Who's this you brought for me to inflict suffering on today?"

A brawny man with a shaved head and bushy moustache strode over to me with his hand outstretched. Normally, I'd cross the street to avoid a guy like that. He was enormous, in all directions. He looked like a wrestler or one of the biker dudes in the parking lot, from the snake tattoo on his forearm to the silver hoop in one ear. His lips widened in a grin, and his eyes glinted menacingly. I shivered. Sam and her mom smiled back at him.

"This is Joe, a friend of Sam and Parker's," said Mrs. Brown. "We call him Jelly. Jelly, this is Henry, the manager of Food Share."

I stuck out my hand and felt it enclosed by a large leathery paw. Henry's handshake almost dislocated my shoulder.

"Very happy to meet you, Jelly," said Henry in his huge voice. "That's an interesting nickname." He raised a gigantic eyebrow. "Long story, eh? Well, never mind. Where's P.B. today?"

"He's out of town — hockey game," said Sam.

"Too bad," said Henry. "Guess I'll have to mistreat his buddy here instead. He looks like he's got some muscle."

He punched my arm and winked at me. "We can always use an extra body this time of year. Come with me, tough guy." He led me off to another room. Henry didn't seem so intimidating anymore but I wondered how much muscle he expected me to have.

"I'll get on with the paperwork," called Mrs. Brown. "Sam will sort and pack boxes."

"Thanks, Rose," shouted back Henry. "You and me," he said, "we'll do the manly stuff — heave boxes around and make rude jokes." He laughed.

It was going to be a strange morning.

The second room in the food bank was almost as big as the first, but here the brown linoleum floor was covered with wooden skids loaded with cardboard boxes. I read some of the handwritten labels stuck to the sides of the boxes. They said things like *spaghetti sauce* and *tuna*.

"This is where we store the food when it comes in," said Henry. "We don't have much room."

I looked up at the stacks of boxes, some already beginning to lean.

"Don't worry," said Henry. "We'll make 'em fit."

I wasn't worried about them fitting. I was worried about them falling — on me.

As the morning went on, my arms ached. I hauled boxes as Sam filled them with cans of food. Henry heaved them up on top of piles that seemed about to collapse, but

JENNIFER MOOK-SANG

nothing shifted. Every so often he'd squint at the writing on the boxes I brought. He muttered something about getting old and needing glasses, so I read the labels for him — *tomato soup, corn, beans.*

I handed Henry another box, and he tossed it way up high on top of the peas. "After twelve years, I'm the king of stacking," he bragged.

Whoa! Twelve years was longer than I'd been alive.

"You must really like working here," I said, leaning over to stretch out my sore spine.

"Sure do. And it's my way of giving back," said Henry. He noticed my puzzled look. "When I arrived in town years ago, I was pretty young. Didn't have too many prospects." He chuckled. "You know, opportunities."

I nodded.

"Food Share helped me get by until I got on my feet. The people who work here don't judge. They get you through the rough spots." The corners of Henry's eyes crinkled when he smiled at me. "As soon as I could, I came back to help out. It's like you kids talk about in school — paying it forward. But I guess I'm paying it back." He chortled at his own joke.

I liked the part about not being judged.

For the next hour and a half, Henry yakked while I lugged boxes. He checked his watch. "Time for our coffee break."

"Um, I don't drink coffee."

"What? If you work at Food Share, you drink coffee — it's a rule." Henry gestured to an open doorway in the corner. "Welcome to Henry's Office and Café," he said. "Hey, Sam," he called, "break time!"

"I am so ready," she said, coming through the door and flopping down on a chair.

Henry's small office held the tiny window I'd seen from the parking lot. Under it stood a huge old-fashioned wooden desk littered with manuals, computer parts and CDs. The hard drive, flat screen monitor and printer all looked brand new.

On the filing cabinet in the corner, the coffee machine hissed as the last drop of steaming brown liquid dripped into the glass carafe. Henry filled four battered ceramic mugs. He took two of them out to the front desk where Sam's mom sat writing in a big book.

Sam said, "Aren't you going to put anything in yours?"

"I don't drink coffee."

"C'mon, give it here. I'll fix it for you." She flung the ends of her multi-coloured scarf over her shoulders and rolled up her sleeves. She put in three heaping spoons of sugar and topped up my mug with cream. She handed it to me, and I looked doubtfully at the thick, sandy-coloured liquid.

"Drink up," she commanded.

I sipped it. It wasn't bad. Sweet . . . Like . . .

Sam caught my eye, and I felt my cheeks flush. I turned away and looked out the door. "What did Henry mean about needing extra people this time of year?" I asked.

"It's almost Thanksgiving. That's when we do our big food drive."

I remembered seeing the bins at the grocery stores, with cans of stew and boxes of macaroni and cheese at the bottom.

Sam continued, "For a few weeks, we're crazy busy organizing all the food that comes in and making sure it gets to where it's needed."

"How often does the food bank do a big collection?"

"The next one will be at Christmas," she said. "Then there's one at Easter."

"What happens if you run out of food in between?"

She shrugged. "Hopefully, we won't."

Just then, there was an awful noise from the main room. It started as a wail then rose in volume and pitch, until my eardrums vibrated. At last, it stopped, and a determined voice sobbed, "I want to go home. Now!"

Sam and I rushed to the door. In the aisle by the front desk stood a little girl with straight black hair, faced off against a woman with a shopping cart.

The woman spoke soothingly. "Addie, we'll be home soon. Mommy just has to get some groceries, then Daddy will come to pick us up."

"I want Daddy to come *now!*" said the little girl.

"Daddy's at an interview, Addie," said another voice. Behind the little girl stood a slightly taller one with the same kind of straight black hair. She tried to take her little sister's hand. "Daddy's coming soon. Soon as he's done."

The mother nodded. "Hop in the cart, baby. It won't be long."

The little girl pulled her hand away from her sister's and stamped her foot. "I'm *not* a baby! I'm *two and free-quarters*. And. I. Want. To. Go. *Home!*"

Uh-oh, this wasn't going well. I edged my way over to the commotion. Everyone was staring at the girls and their mom. Henry stood by looking dazed. Sam's mom got up from behind the desk and gestured toward a toy box on the floor. "Would you like to sit at the little table and play while Mommy shops?"

The smaller girl glared at her. She clutched her mother's leg and opened her mouth to wail again. This *definitely* wasn't going well. I scanned inside the box of well-worn toys and reached for a ragged blue bear with a slightly shredded nose. The little girl glanced over to see what I was doing.

I waggled the stuffed toy in front of her face and squeaked out of the side of my mouth. "Hi! My name's Bear. What's yours?" My lips barely moved. Dad would be proud of me. The girl's eyes opened almost as wide as her mouth. She eyed the bear suspiciously then looked right at me. I gazed off into the distance, all innocent. *Who me?* I thought. *I'm just holding the bear. The bear asked you a question, kid.*

The girl looked back at the decrepit bear and said, "Addie."

I made Bear give a little hop of joy. "That's a great name," he squeaked. "My best friend's name is Addie too.

She's a . . . kitty cat . . . and pink . . . and, uh, she loves to colour. Do you like to colour?" I made Bear talk slow and friendly. I may be an only child but I've had my share of entertaining the smaller cousins at family gatherings.

I held my breath waiting for Addie to answer. I sensed the adults behind me did too, and I tried to pretend they weren't there. The girl considered Bear's question, then she nodded.

Bear shook with excitement. "Hey, you know what? I love to colour too." I made his voice sound as sad as a squeaky bear's could. "I love to colour. But I can't." Bear held up a paw. "I gots no fingers." The girl frowned. He pressed on. "Do you think you could help me hold the crayons?"

Her face full of sympathy, Addie whispered, "Sure, Bear." I placed him in her hands and, as inconspicuously as possible, pulled out a chair for her. She sat down, carefully arranged Bear on the table and asked, "What colour do you want?"

Bear said, "Pink, please." And added, "Um, can your mom shop while we colour?"

"Sure," said Addie.

"Do you think your sister wants to colour with us?" asked Bear.

Addie stuck out her lower lip. "No! Kayla has to go shopping wif Mommy."

Her mom backed away mouthing, "Thank you." The older sister, Kayla, gave me the thumbs-up sign and a wide grin before she followed her mom down the aisle. I caught a glimpse of Sam in the background. She had an odd look on her face.

Oh man, I thought. Now Sam knows about this weird side of me with the bizarre voices and talking animals. This could be embarrassing. But it was too late to do anything but make sure Addie and Bear had a good time together.

* * * * *

"Holy cow!" Sam said afterwards. "I didn't know you could throw your voice like that."

I shook my head. "That wasn't me," I said. "That was the talking bear."

She laughed and relief washed over me. "That was nice of you to play with that girl so her mom could shop."

"Well," I said, "sure beats having to do manual labour with that slave-driver, Henry. I'm delicate, you know, can't take the strain."

I smiled at Sam to make sure she knew I was kidding. She smiled back.

Sam didn't make me feel weird. She made me feel excellent.

* * * * *

When I got home from the food bank, I got out my planner and checked my homework list. At the top was printed: CHOOSE TOPIC FOR SPEECH! I thought of the prize and wished there were some other way to get one. I picked up my money jar and shook it. All I heard was a few pathetic clinks. I tried to convince myself that the competition was silly and I didn't need the tablet anyway. But I knew if I didn't at least try, I wouldn't have any chance of winning. And the sneer on Victoria's face would get bigger.

I got out a sheet of paper and my lucky pen. World peace? Greenpeace? The Nobel Peace Prize? I mulled over world peace but gave up. I had no idea how to achieve world peace, unless it was in a virtual world. I thought about the fun we had at Parker's house, playing games, exchanging insults and beating on each other. I made a list of all the things I knew anything about. I crossed out the ones I wasn't interested in. That narrowed it down.

I wrote the topic sentence in big letters at the top of the page and underlined it twice. I pictured myself playing games online with my friends on my very own tablet and started the outline. I wondered what my dad would say if he knew the topic of my speech.

9

At lunchtime on Monday, Parker dragged me to the student council room. "I need your help."

"Why are we here?" I protested. "We're not even on student council."

"I promised I'd help with the Crazy Hair Day fundraiser, and I forgot all about it. You have to help me make posters and put them up around school," he said. "They need to be done by this afternoon."

"Sam asked you to do this?"

His answer was muffled as he rummaged in the cupboard for paper and markers.

When he emerged, he was smiling and saying, "How could I say no?"

Maybe Sam would be impressed that I got involved in my school community.

It was like the old days when Parker and I did class projects together. We tried to come up with as many different ideas as we could for the posters, even if they sounded ridiculous. We brainstormed stuff like taking pictures of the teachers and Photoshopping outrageous hairstyles on them, or making glow-in-the-dark posters on fluorescent paper.

I started making cartoons of the teachers. Parker was impressed. "Man, I wish I could draw like that." He cut some of the fluorescent paper into strips for hair and glued them to the pictures. He curled the strips for the curly-haired teachers and made a goofy spiky hair-do for Ms Longo. Mrs. Muddgrove got dreadlocks. Next, I drew pictures of the student council executive. There was Victoria standing in the middle with a mess of wavy hair, Becky with long, straight blond hair and Elsa with her super-short hairstyle. I cut out a frilly green moustache from construction paper and started to tape it on Victoria's picture. Parker stopped me and laughed. "You don't want to get in *more* trouble with Victoria, do you?"

It was tempting.

"Jelly," said Parker, as we put away the markers, "Sam wanted me to ask if you can help again at the food bank on Saturday."

Another opportunity to show Sam how helpful and involved I could be?

"Sure, why not?"

As we stuck the posters to the walls, Parker asked, "Did you decide on your speech yet?"

"I don't know if it's any good, but I wrote something," I replied. "The worst thing about giving a speech is feeling everyone's eyes on me while I say it. Then I mess up even more."

"Jelly, everyone messes up," Parker said. "I fell down a lot when I was learning how to skate. Now look at me. I'm a world-class goalie."

"Sure, sure," I said, agreeably. If confidence made a goalie, then Parker was galaxy-class.

"Besides, you have other things you're good at, like drawing, and . . ." he grinned at me, "Sam's still going on about the talking bear."

I grinned back. He was right, of course. No one's perfect, and everyone has *something* they're good at. But I really wished my talent was a speech-making superpower.

* * * * *

The next few days at school were a blur of writing and rewriting. I went on the Internet and found articles to help fill in the spaces of my outline. Ms Mitrovika gave us tips, and everyone polished their presentations.

The writing and the memorizing were not so bad. But the presenting part — well, I just had to imagine one person looking at me and I got all sweaty.

Each year, I'd passed the speech project simply because I got a good mark on the written part. I knew the things you're *supposed* to do when you're making a speech. But I couldn't actually *do* them. All through school, my teachers said, "Joe, you know the answer. Just speak up." They sometimes called on me even though I didn't put my hand up, to see if they could surprise the answer out of me. It never worked.

Now, I tried not to listen while my classmates recited their speeches to each other because it made me nervous. I took the long way round to my classes so I wouldn't see the tablet winking at me in the front hallway. I knew I should be rehearsing but I convinced myself I had lots of time.

Even though Parker was still "working" on his speech, he seemed to spend an awful lot of time in the student council room. I helped him count money collected from Crazy Hair Day and we made more posters for the next month's cookie sale. I hoped Sam would notice what I was doing for the worthy causes.

At the end of two weeks of preparation, I had no idea if my speech was any good. I hadn't even read it out loud yet — even to myself.

10

"I'd have asked some other melonhead to help," said Sam, "but you already know what to do, Jelly."

"*Other* melonhead?" I tried to look offended but found myself smiling instead. Parker was away again and Sam needed *me* at the food bank.

This Saturday morning, we worked at top speed sorting cans and stacking boxes. Henry wanted everything organized when the big gang of volunteers came to fill up the Thanksgiving hampers.

I missed the drama of last time and wondered if I'd see Addie and Kayla. Sam teased me about being Mr. Popular with small children. The joking around made me feel like I could ask her about something that was bugging me.

"Sam, why do you think Victoria's so popular?"

"Well . . . she's smart and helpful and . . ." Sam hesitated. "She's nice?"

"Lots of people are like that. Besides, you know Victoria's not nice to *everyone*."

"Okay, she's nice to *some* people," admitted Sam. "I suppose if you get in her way or don't treat her like she's special, she can be a bit mean."

"No kidding. So why does anyone want to hang around with her?"

Sam frowned. "It's because, if you're on the wrong side of Victoria, your other friends won't want to be friends with you."

I threw my hands in the air. "Why not?"

"Because then she won't be friends with *them*."

"So, if you want any friends at all, you have to be friends with Victoria?"

"Yup," she said. "That's it."

I will never understand girls.

I had one more question for Sam. "You're not really one of her friends, are you?"

Sam laughed. "No. Too much drama," she said. "But I try to stay on her good side because we have to work together for student council."

By the time coffee break rolled around, my arms felt like they were kilometres long. I helped Sam finish one last box of cans, and Henry came over. He blocked out the light and twirled one end of his large moustache. "Jelly, I have a big favour to ask you."

"Sure, Henry. What is it?" I hoped it didn't have anything to do with cleaning out the produce bins.

Mrs. Brown came by and handed Henry a bunch of papers. "Before you chat, Henry, give this a quick read through and sign it for me."

Henry flipped through the stack. He drew a careful *H* and a long scrawl beside the *X* marked on the last page. Mrs. Brown took the papers and the pen and headed back to the front desk.

Henry seemed serious for a change. "Mrs. Brown tells me you know something about computers."

"Something?" exclaimed Sam. "Jelly knows *everything* about computers."

Henry nodded. "A while back, we got a brand new one. It was supposed to make my life easier with the number-crunching and all. But I didn't have time . . ."

Halfway back to the front desk, Sam's mom turned. "Don't feel bad, Henry," she said. "Some of us are more used to old-fashioned technology." She held up her pen and chuckled.

"I gave it my best shot," continued Henry. "I even went to classes on how to use the thing. But I still don't know which plug goes into the wall."

"Once it's plugged in," I asked, working hard not to laugh, "what does it have to do?"

Henry started a long spiel about stakeholders, funding and boards of directors. My brain glazed over. From the look on Sam's face, she understood as much as I did — zippo. Henry blabbed on about percentages, statistics and data.

"Wait a minute!" I said. "You mean you want to keep track of the people who come in and use Food Share?"

"Yeah. We used to do that on the old computer but it crashed. I need the numbers to show the people who help us with funding why we need their support," Henry explained.

Mrs. Brown called over from the front desk, "Henry's very persuasive. Since he started making these presentations, we've had lots more businesses sign up to help us."

"But I can't do anything without the facts to back me up," said Henry.

"Why don't you get the same program you had before and keep putting the numbers in like you used to?" I asked.

Henry shook his head. "It's really old. Even if we could still get a copy of that program, it can't sort the figures the way the board of directors wants them now."

It didn't sound too hard. Take the data from one computer and put it into another computer. Then use a new program to arrange the numbers in a new way.

"I'll do it," I said.

"You will? That's great!" Then Henry hesitated. "But . . ."

"Don't worry. I know what I'm doing."

"That's not it," said Henry. "The thing is, we don't have much money to pay you."

Pay me? I thought I had a sweet deal getting to play around on a computer. But he was right. I should get a more substantial reward for my efforts. Genius does have a price.

Sam was already saying, "I'm sure Jelly doesn't want . . ."

I spoke up. "Consultants make about a hundred dollars an hour for this kind of thing." I scratched my head.

Henry sighed. "A hundred an hour. We don't have —"

"Yeah, it's complicated. It could get ugly. Once I transfer the data, I'd have to build and load a user-friendly, web-based, front-end . . ."

"Huh?" They both stared at me.

". . . for a client database." I nodded as if they knew exactly what I was talking about. "You know, graphical user interface — GUI."

"I don't know," said Henry, his large brow furrowed. "Gooey front-end loaders and such. Sounds a little over our budget."

"Hmm." I stroked my chin like I'd seen the lawyers do on TV. "Let's see, maybe I can make you an offer."

Sam gazed at me with narrowed eyes. I walked over to the desk and wrote on a piece of paper. I folded it and handed it to Henry. He opened it up and took his time reading it. Then he nodded and shook my hand. "I appreciate this, Jelly," he said. "We've got a deal."

Sam couldn't hold it in anymore. She grabbed the paper out of Henry's hand and said, "I can't believe you're making him pay you, you . . ." She read what I'd written and frowned in confusion. ". . . You want hot chocolate? With marshmallows?"

I smirked at her, and she whacked me on the shoulder. Hard.

"Thank goodness," she said. "I was starting to think you were a money-grubbing melonhead."

Henry waved a hand at his office where the remains of the old computer were stuffed into a cardboard box on the floor and pieces of the new one were scattered on the desk.

"Okay, Jelly," he said. "It's all yours."

I didn't feel tired anymore. A computer to play with, a problem to solve and hot chocolate instead of coffee. Awesome! Best of all, I liked the way Sam was looking at me, all happy and admiring.

11

After spending Saturday morning at Food Share, I had the rest of the weekend to panic about my speech. It was written but presentations began on Monday. I needed serious help, and the one person I could count on was at a hockey tournament all day. On Sunday morning, after I ate a bowl of cereal, I phoned Parker and asked him to come over.

"I'd do anything to get away from here," he said. "But I'm stuck in my room till my homework's done." His voice suddenly got cheery. "Hey, why don't you come to my house?"

I grabbed my speech and hurried over.

Parker sat in front of a computer game.

"Gooberface," I said. "I see you're working hard."

"And if by working hard you mean hardly working, you'd be right, Jellyface."

I bumped his fist with mine.

"Who's playing Clash today?" I asked.

Clash was an online game, much like Rebel Ruckus but played with people on the Internet.

"I'm playing with a bunch of kids in Korea," he said. "Look at this cool smiley face — they have the best emojis."

"I'm here to practise my butt-kicking speech-making skills," I reminded him.

"Yeah, yeah." Parker looked up briefly, then clicked energetically with his mouse. "I'll just collect my gold coins first."

I cleared my throat ominously.

His fingers flew over the keyboard. "Okay, okay, I'm shutting down."

The monitor went black as he swung around in his chair to face me. "Let's hear that speech."

Suddenly, my palms were clammy. *It's P.B.*, I said to myself. *My good friend, Goober. He's not going to laugh at me.*

I took a deep breath and reminded myself to focus on the audience. *The audience is dying to hear what you have to say.*

"I haven't got all day," grumbled the audience. "I've got my own speech to work on. And a bunch of other stuff too." Parker glanced longingly at his computer. "C'mon, Jelly, start talking."

I aimed for a smooth, deep voice. Expressive and melodious. But the first words came out in a squeaky rush.

"Whoa, slow down," said Parker. He waved his hands at me. "Think about your motivation. Imagine you're trying to convince your parents to get you a new computer game."

I pictured Dad standing in front of me and managed to get to the end of my speech.

"Dig your topic," Parker said. "Do it again, but don't stare at your notes. Look up at me now and then, and smile when you talk. Like this." His grin revealed a double row of shiny braces. He squinted his eyes almost shut and his rosy cheeks grew even rounder. With his fluffy head of hair, he looked like an insane clown.

"So, my motivation here is — what?" I asked. "To send everyone screaming for the exits?"

"Just Victoria," said Parker the clown. He smacked me in the arm. "Don't worry, you'll do fine."

I could almost believe him. Parker's never lied to me. Like when he told me I wouldn't get some horrible disease if I stepped on the algae-covered rocks at the lake, or the time he said I'd have fun if I went to Milli Wilson's birthday.

Parker made me do hand gestures. I knew I'd never be able to use them on speech day; I'd be lucky to remember "slowly and clearly." But, I figured the more I did in practice, the better my chances of not sounding like a total imbecile in front of my class. Rehearsing was even less pleasant than I'd thought.

Parker's dad appeared at the door and said, "P.B., I told you to finish your homework before you had friends over."

"Right," said Parker. "I *am* working. Um, Jelly and I are helping each other with speeches. Plus, I needed him to check our Internet connection. It's been super slow. I hope he can fix it." He looked at his dad, wide-eyed. "I can't do research without the Internet."

Mr. Brown said, "Thanks, Jelly. Seems like something's always messed up on this computer." He smiled. "I think instead of an Apple, we got a lemon."

I chuckled politely.

"Lucky for us your dad taught you so much about computers," said Mr. Brown.

I didn't correct him. My dad was in the business, but besides letting me have a computer after years of begging, he hadn't taught me much. He left his how-to-fix and how-to-program computer books around the house and I borrowed them.

After his dad left, I pushed Parker off the chair and sped up their Internet connection. Then we tried to find some stuff on the web to use for his speech.

He was certain that rock 'n' roll was dead and that rap had killed it. But there was no evidence to support his theory. I told him it would have to come from his heart. When Parker's gung-ho about something, he takes off like a race car on speed boost.

In the end, he had me convinced that rap had taken a lightsaber and plunged it through the heart of rock 'n' roll.

12

On Monday all the speeches were handed in. Ms Mitrovika said, "Everybody take a number from the hat to see who goes first."

She came around with a pointy Robin Hood thing with a feather in it. I hated that hat. It reminded me of the lame school theme and the fact that I had to wear one last year for the school play, even though I was only a stagehand. I reached in and drew last place, right after Victoria.

Ms Mitrovika said, "I can hardly wait to hear your wonderful speeches. Good luck, everyone."

It took days to get through all the presentations. I alternated between wishing it was over and being relieved it wasn't my turn yet.

This year's speeches were better than usual. The possibility of winning that awesome prize meant no one talked less than the minimum time and almost everyone had some kind of visual aid. Guess who had the most visual aids?

Her mother dropped off a gigantic three-fold poster, and Victoria set it up in the back of the classroom. We could read about the conservation of biodiversity in South America whenever we had a spare moment. When her turn came, she opened her laptop and rolled down the large white screen at the front of the room. Then she snapped her fingers for someone to dim the lights and started her PowerPoint presentation.

Victoria's statistics and charts were excellent. But her presentation skills were unbelievable. She made everyone in the room feel like she was talking right to them. She lowered her voice when she told us the little spotted cat was almost extinct because of hunters, and because farmers cut down their forest homes to make space for coffee plantations. She used her finger to jab guilt into the soul of any coffee drinker in the room. I heard a few sniffles then.

Though I tried not to care, I was convinced that every plant and animal deserved a place in the world. I found myself wishing Victoria would tell us what we could do to make a difference, besides making donations. Instead, she handed out flyers for people to take home and relive the experience. Many of them ended up in the recycling bin, but I kept mine. I thought I'd ask Henry where his coffee beans came from.

As Victoria packed up, I looked at the clock. Ten minutes till the end of class. I prayed she'd take her time and the bell would go before it could be my turn. After her impossibly perfect speech, anyone would sound terrible. But, with seven minutes left in the period, Ms Mitrovika called out, "And now, we'll hear from our last speaker. Joe . . ." Icy fingers wrapped around my stomach and gave a little squeeze.

This was it. I picked up my stack of cue cards and tried to picture the shiny tablet in the display case. *It's just acting*, I told myself. I'm going to pretend to be someone who can give a speech. I stood on vibrating legs and forced myself to walk to the front of the room. My hands shook so hard I almost dropped the cards. I stumbled behind the teacher's desk and was glad to have something between me and the class.

I blinked into the sea of faces. Some were whispering to each other or passing notes. Others were surreptitiously scribbling in their math books, desperately trying to get their homework done before the next class. Victoria smirked. Ms Mitrovika smiled encouragingly and nodded at me to begin.

I remembered what Parker had said. "The most important thing is to breathe out. The in-breaths take care of themselves." I could barely remember the topic of my speech but I exhaled and took a deep breath.

"Good afternoon, Ms Mitrovika and fellow students," I squeaked.

Victoria snorted.

My face burned but I looked at my first cue card and all the strategies Ms Mitrovika had been drilling into us came spilling out. "My name is Joe Miles. Today, I would like to tell you about the redeeming qualities of video games."

It was as if someone had pushed the pause button. The chatter stopped. All eyes turned on me and I felt a flood of alarm. *Think about Parker,* I told myself. *Pretend he's the only one sitting out there.* It was hard, but I imagined Parker sitting in the front row. *Do the Darth Vader voice,* he was saying. I forced James Earl Jones into my vocal cords and continued in my deepest tone.

"Lots of people tell us why we shouldn't play video games. Child psychologists say the games isolate us, destroy our social skills, dull our creativity and make us fat."

Ms Mitrovika scribbled something in her marking book.

"Well, *I* say that's a load of junk. *And* I have research to back me up. This research was done by people with important letters after their names, like psychologists, neurobiologists and even . . ." I paused and went deep into my diaphragm, "The National Institute of Health."

"Yeah, you go, Jelly," shouted Jeff Davies in the back. Everyone laughed, except Victoria. I started to breathe easier. I cleared my throat — and squeaked again. This time Victoria snorted even louder. I pictured Parker and me playing Journey to Outer Zed on my new tablet and pressed on.

"Video games are a virtual place to hang out. We talk, play and work with each other toward a goal — like finding the treasure or solving the puzzle. We share information, help one another and practise our leadership skills."

Ms Mitrovika would like that one — she was always going on about leadership.

"Video games help kids feel comfortable with technology. We all know how to use a computer mouse. But my dad says it took him a whole week to get the hang of it."

Everyone nodded. I told them how video games boosted self-confidence and memory; improved reading, math and problem-solving. Surgeons who played video games were faster and more precise than surgeons who didn't. I mentioned all the games that encouraged people to exercise and get fit while having fun.

It was the longest five minutes of my life.

"In conclusion," I said, "video games aren't all bad.

And there *are* ways to figure out if you're spending too much time gaming." I listed them: "One, you're cranky all the time. Two, you can't remember your friends' names in real life. And three, you haven't had a shower in four days." I paused. "Of course, all these things might also be true if you were preparing for a speech competition. Thank you."

Silence.

For one long moment, no one even blinked. Then there was an explosion of laughter and applause. All the boys and a few of the girls got to their feet and cheered. Ms Mitrovika smiled and clapped her fingertips together. Victoria glared and pouted.

The bell rang and I felt like I'd defeated the final boss in Rebel Ruckus. As I gathered my cards, I thought I saw Victoria whisper something to Becky and look in my direction.

After class, people stopped me in the hall and asked me to email them copies of my speech so they could convince their parents to let them play more video games. That kind of attention felt awkward but nice.

Parker strolled by with Sam and put his hand up for a high-five. "Nice work, Jelly. You rock!"

"How do you know already?"

Sam grinned and held up her cellphone. "You're this morning's hot topic."

"How did *your* speeches go?" I asked.

Sam shrugged. "You never really know till they announce the class winners at assembly."

"So we've still got hope," said Parker.

Sam looked at me. "It sounds like you've sent a callout to Victoria."

Yeah, I guess Victoria might think I was sending some kind of challenge. That reminded me of something. "You're on student council, right, Sam? How come they've never organized a fundraiser for the food bank?"

Sam drew her eyebrows together and chewed her lip. "That's a good question."

"Hasn't anyone ever asked about doing a food drive?"

"Well, sure. I have, a few times. But . . ."

"But what?"

"Well, you know, council's always busy doing stuff for children in Africa, or collecting money for endangered animals . . ."

Oh, I got it. The stuff Victoria the council president was interested in. Stuff that sounded big and important.

A couple of guys from my class came up to me and

slapped my palm. One of them said, "Wow, do you ever know a lot about gaming. That was the best speech ever."

Sam gave me a sideways look and smiled. While I took down their email addresses, she went to hip hop practice and Parker took off to help the phys. ed. teacher in the gym.

I managed to sneak away into the computer lab for some quiet time. But Mr. Chan found me and sent me outside to "get some fresh air and sunshine, young man."

Busted. He told me to toss a ball around with my friends. I thought of the goons on the playground tossing around the smaller kids while the on-duty teacher's back was turned and decided to avoid the crowds. I headed over to the little kids' part of the schoolyard. It was better supervised, quieter, calmer.

I loped along, minding my own business, when I heard, "Hey, Smelly-Jelly," followed by giggles.

Oh no. Victoria. And she had Elsa and Becky with her. They came straight over to me.

"All alone?" Victoria asked. "Oh, such a pity, you don't have any friends." She tilted her head to one side. "Except Parker. And he only lets you hang around with him because he feels sorry for you."

I gritted my teeth and walked away.

"I feel a little sorry for you too," she continued, following me. "It was tough giving that video game speech, eh?

All those people staring at you. Makes you feel nauseous just thinking about it, doesn't it?"

Nauseous was the word all right. It was hard to ignore Victoria's mocking voice. I changed direction and walked faster, but I couldn't shake them.

"Well, aren't you going to say something?" Victoria demanded.

I really wanted to tell her where to go, but that would make things worse.

"You think you're so great, don't you?" Her voice went louder with each sentence. "You want people to think you're so brilliant you don't even have to answer questions. But you're not smart — you're a coward — *that's* why you won't put your hand up in class."

Becky snickered.

"Well, don't worry," said Victoria. "You won't have to give that speech again. Not only was it crappy, but now everyone knows you stole the whole thing from the Internet." She was beside me now and shook her head sadly. "Cheaters don't win, Smelly."

I stopped walking. "What are you talking about?"

Victoria gave me an innocent look. "Well, that's what I heard on the playground."

"Who's telling those lies?" I blurted out.

The smug expression on her face was all the answer I needed.

"Awww, it's too bad for you, Smelly-Jelly," said Victoria. "But the voters have a right to know the whole story."

Another voice broke through the fog of anger and amazement beginning to form in my head.

"Hey! Hey, you!"

I turned, and there was one of the girls from the food bank. The older one. What was her name? Kayla. She gave me a big smile. "Hey, you're that boy with the bear."

Victoria's eyes widened as she leaned in toward us.

"Hi, Kayla," I said.

"Hi. How's Bear?"

"He's good," I said. I couldn't help smiling. "He's still colouring."

"Mom says me and Addie can come back to the food bank and visit you and him soon."

"Um, that's good."

"Food bank!" Victoria broke in. "What were you doing at the food bank?"

"We get food there, silly," said Kayla, patiently. "That's why it's called a food bank."

Victoria shook her head in irritation. She stared scornfully at me. "Why were *you* there?"

I ignored her.

"Hey," said Kayla to me, "what's your name, anyway?"

"Jelly . . . Joe," I said.

"Jelly-Joe. That's a cool name."

Victoria wasn't so easily distracted. "Hey, kid, I was talking to loser-boy. Get lost."

"He's *my* friend. I can talk to him if I want." Kayla took my hand. "Right, Jelly-Joe?"

Before I could answer, Victoria said, "Get out of here, you baby!"

"Don't. Call. Me. *Baby!*" shouted Kayla.

"Baby," crooned Victoria.

Kayla's face creased and her bottom lip trembled.

My hands curled into fists. "Hey!" I said. "Don't talk to her like that."

"I'll talk to her how I want," said Victoria. "Who's going to stop me? You? You jellyfish? You're just a spineless jelly-fish." Victoria leaned over me and jeered, "You're nothing but a loser, cheater, smelly, jelly, fish."

Inside my head something snapped. Everything turned red. I unclenched my fists, and without a thought, my hands shot out and pushed Victoria on the shoulders. Not hard. Just enough to shake her up. Make her stop talking.

Her eyes grew big and her mouth dropped open. Then, as if in slow motion, she started to tip back. Her arms began to wave in slow, wide circles, then faster and faster. She took a few steps backwards, still flailing. Then slowly, slowly, frame-by-flip-book-frame, she crumpled and sat down with a gentle bump. Her mouth was a big O.

Victoria sat there looking startled. Then her mouth turned down. She scrunched up her face and let out a big *"WAAAAAAH!!!"* She took a breath and started yelling, *"Help! Help me! I'm hurt. Ohh, I can't get up. Somebody help me!"*

Elsa and Becky reached to help her up but she brushed off their hands.

Kayla went over and shook Victoria by the shoulder. "Stop it. You're not hurt. Be quiet."

But she wouldn't stop. Even when a collection of kids gathered around us, all pushing to see what had happened, she kept up the commotion. A teacher finally noticed the rowdy mob in the corner of the kiddie playground and trotted over. Victoria waited till he was close, pointed an accusing finger at me and said, "He did it. He hit me and pushed me down."

She started sobbing. Only then did she let herself be helped up and taken, limping, to the office. The teacher nodded at me to follow them. Becky tagged along. Elsa had disappeared.

"You're going to get it now," Becky muttered under her breath.

I knew it. Fresh air and sunshine were bad for my health.

14

Victoria and I sat in hard plastic chairs on opposite sides of the principal's office door. Becky stood beside Victoria, patting her shoulder and making sympathetic noises. Though she tried very hard, Victoria couldn't find any actual scrapes or bruises to show the teacher, so he'd gone to return the first-aid kit.

Victoria and Becky scowled at me. I wondered what my mom was going to think when she got another call from school about her son the bully. I thought back to when I'd gotten in trouble on the bus. Even though they knew all about Spencer the brat, Mom and Dad had been pretty angry with me. At least this victim was bigger than me. But she was a girl. And who was the principal going to believe? Me? Or the person most likely to be voted Student of the Year?

Mrs. Muddgrove came out of her office and ushered us in. I told my side of the story, and Victoria and Becky told hers. There was no witness for me. They made me sound like a rude, socially challenged halfwit who went around beating up helpless girls on the playground. I resigned myself to a worse fate than writing letters of apology.

There was a tap on the door. The teacher from the playground was back, and behind him was Kayla. "Excuse me, Mrs. Muddgrove, this little one says she saw the altercation and wants to say something about it." He pushed Kayla gently into the room.

"Well hello, young lady," said Mrs. Muddgrove, sounding surprised. "It's Kayla, isn't it?"

Kayla stared at her feet and nodded. Eventually she said, "I was talking to my friend, er, Jelly-Joe. And that girl," Kayla pointed at Victoria, "called me a name. Then, um, she started teasing me and wouldn't stop when Jelly-Joe told her to."

Mrs. Muddgrove turned to Victoria and Becky and raised her eyebrows. They looked at their knees.

Kayla pointed at Victoria again, "Then she yelled at him and called him a lot of mean names. Then he pushed her, just a little bit, and she fell over, right on her butt. Um, that's all."

Victoria glared at Kayla and shook her head. Becky still contemplated her knees.

Mrs. Muddgrove said, "Hmm." Then she asked Kayla, "How do you know Joe?"

"He's my friend from the food bank. Can I go and play now?"

Mrs. Muddgrove nodded and motioned for Becky to leave too. I opened the door for them and whispered, "Thanks," to Kayla. She gave me a little wave and ran down the hall. Becky walked a little way and waited for Victoria.

When I sat down again, Mrs. Muddgrove's lips were pressed tightly together. She tapped her fingers on the desk and said, "It appears that you're both responsible in this incident. Therefore, you'll share the detention."

I groaned inside. I'd rather go without using a computer for a month than share anything with Victoria. We apologized to each other, and I shook hands as sincerely as possible.

As we went out, the principal said, "Joe, I'm afraid you've had too many escapades like this lately. I should warn you that if something like this happens again, you will be facing suspension." And with those chilling words she closed the door.

I saw Victoria smile as she walked away to join Becky. I thought of what my parents would do to me if I was ever

suspended. A vision of the tablet danced into my head —
with a big *X* through it.

* * * * *

Victoria and I spent recess that afternoon and the next
morning helping Ms Longo shelve books in the library.
All the activity at the food bank had been good practice
for bending over to return the picture books that were
at floor level. Victoria ignored me, thank goodness. She
talked endlessly to Ms Longo about how she was going to
improve her speech for the "real" judges.

When we ran out of books to put away, Ms Longo
assigned us the dictionary. She told us to start with *A* and
make up a sentence for each word. I entertained myself
by writing:

A — Victoria is A dweeb.

AA — The AA (Automobile Association) has made a
request to the city for "Victoria Crossing" warning signs.

AARDVARK — Like the AARDVARK, Victoria has
long ears and a snout.

ABACK — I was taken ABACK by Victoria's long ears
and snout.

ABACUS — The children used an ABACUS to count
the many nose hairs on Victoria's snout.

ABALONE — The shell of the ABALONE is impervi-
ous to Victoria's hairy snout.

I got all the way to ABSCESS — The ABSCESS on Victoria's snout is filled with pus — when the bell sounded.

I saw with dismay that Victoria was giving her paper to the librarian. Now Ms Longo was on her way over to collect mine. I hadn't thought anyone would see my work. I thought she was just keeping us bored and punished. I contemplated eating it, but it was a full sheet. I folded it in half and handed it over. *Yikes!* She unfolded it. Ms Longo started to read and her eyebrows shot up.

I knew I was in trouble now. I saw the edges of her lips quiver. I wondered if this could count toward suspension. Worse, out of the corner of my eye, I could see Victoria coming toward us. My heart dropped to the pit of my stomach. Victoria stood quietly beside the librarian and peered at my list. Ms Longo came to the end and shook her head. There'd been a lot of head shaking lately.

"Hey!" Victoria said. Her eyes glittered. "Wait till Mrs. Muddgrove sees that. You're gonna get it now."

Ms Longo seemed surprised to see Victoria standing there. She sighed and looked at me. "Joe?" she asked. "What do you have to say for yourself?"

I thought as fast as I could. I opened my mouth. Nothing came out but I could taste panic.

Victoria made a *pfft* of exasperation. "You know that's really inappropriate, Ms Longo. That is completely disrespectful to me. You have to show it to the principal."

"*I* will deal with this," said Ms Longo. "Victoria, you are dismissed."

Victoria scowled at both of us as she strode to the door.

I managed to find my voice. "Ms Longo, I'm sorry about that list. I didn't know I had to hand it in. Please, Ms Longo. If Mrs. Muddgrove sees that she'll suspend me."

Ms Longo frowned at me for a long time while I held my breath. I felt the sweat beading up on the back of my neck. Then she said, "Everyone makes mistakes, Joe." She folded my sheet of paper in half and tucked it into her desk drawer. "Let's file this under 'experience,' and I don't want to see you in detention again."

I forced myself to meet her eyes and nodded my head.

"You can go now," Ms Longo said to me. "Try to stay out of trouble."

Of course I *was* trying to stay out of trouble. But unfortunately, these days, trouble seemed to be lying in puddles all around me.

As I turned, Ms Longo said, "Oh, Joe, I've been meaning to tell you. I sent your drawing off for the school board contest."

I nodded. I remembered the poster I drew for my I-bullied-my-friend-Spencer detention. But I didn't care about some art contest when I barely had one life left before I might be kicked out of school.

15

I'd served my punishment for pushing Victoria. But it wasn't over yet. I still had to deal with the nasty gossip she'd started about my speech. If my classmates thought I'd cheated, they wouldn't vote for me. Yesterday, they'd been all over me about my video game speech. Today, no one even said hi. I caught people stealing curious glances at me and then turning away. I could only imagine what they were saying.

My head ached. Maybe it would be easier to forget the whole thing.

But it wasn't just about the speech contest and the prize anymore. Victoria had been right about one thing. Other kids thought I was smart. And I was proud of that, even though I didn't show off like some people. If they thought I'd cheated, they'd always wonder about me. My whole reputation was at stake.

I needed to talk to Parker. At the next recess, I found him and Sam hanging the posters I'd drawn for the cookie fundraiser. Sam gave me a worried little smile.

"It's all over the school, dude," Parker said. "Your votes are toast."

"What can I do?"

"I don't know." Even the eternally optimistic Parker couldn't think of a solution. He smoothed a drawing of a chocolate chip cookie with legs and stuck it to the wall with tape. "The voting's tomorrow. It's impossible to prove to everyone that you wrote your own speech."

"*You* know I didn't cheat, right, P.B.?"

"Well . . . I guess . . ." He stood there with his big hands hanging down by his big sides.

Sam looked at her brother, shocked.

"What do you mean, you *guess?*" My voice was surprisingly loud.

"You *could* have copied," he explained. "You're smart. You're good at finding stuff on the computer." He wouldn't look me in the eye. "You really wanted to beat Victoria."

I couldn't believe it. I turned and walked away. I heard footsteps, and Sam caught up with me.

"P.B.'s crazy," she said. "I know there's no way you'd cheat. For crying out loud, if you accidentally saw the answers to a quiz, you'd report yourself to the teacher."

I stopped and stared at her. "That's it!"

"That's what?"

"Sam, you have to report me to the office."

Her mouth fell open. "You're crazier than my brother!"

"I have a plan. But we have to do it now or it'll be too late."

I explained my idea as we hurried down the hall.

She was not the most willing accomplice. "No way, Jelly! I can't do that. What if it backfires? What if I get you in worse trouble?"

"Nothing could be worse than this."

* * * * *

I stood outside the receptionist's door while Sam stormed into the main office and demanded to talk to the principal. When she found out Mrs. Muddgrove was in a meeting, she insisted on seeing the vice principal, Mr. Bochek. He came out of his room to see what the noise was about. He took Sam inside and closed the door. I beat it down the hall and waited. After a few minutes, Sam walked by and nodded without looking at me before she headed out the door to the playground.

When the PA crackled, "Joe Miles to the office. Joseph

Miles to the office, please," I walked in, butterflies in my stomach.

Mr. Bochek frowned as he peered at me from across his desk. "There's been an official complaint, Joe." He looked confused. "Someone is very angry that you might have copied your speech from the Internet. Do you have anything to say about that?"

I shook my head and tried to look guilty.

Mr. Bochek seemed even more bewildered. "Joe, you've been getting into a lot of trouble lately. Is something wrong? Is everything okay at home?"

I shrugged my shoulders and gazed at the middle of his tie.

"You're a good student," said Mr. Bochek. "I was hoping you'd tell me this was all a misunderstanding and we could let it go." He looked at me for a moment, then he sighed. "I'll have to call your parents and get this sorted out." He made some notes on the pad on his desk. "Come back and see me after your last class."

By the middle of the afternoon, the rumours had me involved with an underworld mob of Internet writers who sold essays in exchange for the souls of young gamers. Word was, the gamers then had to play forever to earn level-ups and free items for the mob.

At the end of the day, I reported back to Mr. Bochek. He told me he'd phoned my parents and asked them to come to school with me after dinner. "Bring all your notes and a list of your sources," he said.

This was exactly what I wanted, but my insides shook. Even though it was fake trouble, I'd never been in this much trouble before. And what if, at the end of it all, they still didn't believe me? I'd be out of the competition. But worse, everyone would think I was stupid and a cheat.

16

My parents' reactions were predictable.

Dad said, "What on earth is going on with you?"

"Oh, Joe," said my mom. "How could you get into so much trouble in such a short time?"

I could see her point. I had smacked a kid on the bus, and I'd pushed over a girl on the playground. But . . . "I didn't cheat on my speech," I insisted. "I can prove it. Honest."

They looked at me, tight-lipped. Then Dad said, "Well, Joe, I can't think of any reason you'd need to cheat, so I'll keep an open mind."

"Why would anyone start such a mean rumour?" Mom said.

* * * * *

After dinner, I collected my notes and the bibliography of the websites I'd visited for my speech. I came downstairs and sat beside Roger. I put my hand in his back. He turned his head toward me and raised his eyebrows.

"Wish me luck, Roger."

"Luck," was all he said.

Real helpful.

My parents drove me back to school.

Mrs. Muddgrove and Mr. Bochek waited in the office. After the handshaking and so on were done, my parents listened while the accusation against me was read out from an official-looking paper. It didn't take more than half a minute, but by the end, my stomach was clenched and I found it hard to breathe.

Mom asked, "Who made this complaint about Joe?"

"I can tell you it was a student. However, we cannot reveal their name," said Mr. Bochek.

I laid out my papers on the desk with trembling hands. Mrs. Muddgrove shuffled through them and handed the stack to Mr. Bochek, who went through every page. He got on his computer and checked my website references. Dad leaned over and squinted at the screen.

It felt like forever, but when he was done Mr. Bochek said, "Well, this all seems to be in order. I don't find any evidence of plagiarism here."

My parents and I breathed a sigh of relief.

Mrs. Muddgrove leaned across the desk. "Joseph, do you have any idea who might have started this gossip about you?"

I shook my head.

"Well," she said, standing up, "I'm sorry to have put you through all this. But we have to follow up on any specific allegation that comes to the office. I'll clear this up first thing tomorrow."

On the way home, Dad said, "Jelly, I'd like to see that speech you wrote."

I printed off a copy and left it on his side of the desk in the study.

* * * * *

The next morning, I got on the bus and sat beside Spencer. I sure didn't feel like sitting beside Parker. Parker glanced at us when he got on the bus, then headed for the back. It was a quiet ride.

At school, Sam told me the talk was that I got hauled down to the office for being a big fat fraud. There were whispers of suspension, and even expulsion. I prayed the principal wouldn't forget her promise to clear everything up.

It was torture sitting in class listening to the murmurs around me. The bell rang and we stood for the national anthem. When it was over, the speaker crackled as Mrs. Muddgrove came on the PA and cleared her throat. "It has come to the attention of the administration that a senior student has been accused of cheating," she said.

I could feel everyone's eyes dart over to me.

Mrs. Muddgrove's voice continued, "I'd like to announce that the matter has been thoroughly investigated by Mr. Bochek and myself, and there is absolutely no truth to that story." There was a collective gasp. "However, we will be looking further into the matter to find out who started the rumour." I watched Victoria's shoulders tense as she faced front.

It was official. My reputation was clean. I'd won this battle. And after the voting this afternoon, I still had a chance to win the war.

* * * * *

I was no longer in the running for the title of School's Biggest Cheat. But my best friend was being weird, and I didn't know if my speech was good enough. Sure, it got lots of applause but it might not be serious enough to win the contest.

I slumped along through the schoolyard, hoping to find a quiet spot to ponder my much-too-eventful life. I rounded the corner of the kiddie playground when I heard a familiar voice.

It was Kayla, as loud as ever. She was talking to a bunch of little kids standing in a circle around her.

One girl called out, "But why do you go to the food bank. Is your family poor?"

"Yeah," said a boy. "Why doesn't your dad work like the other dads? Is he lazy?"

The hairs on the back of my neck rose and I froze. I tried to think what I could do. But Kayla didn't seem upset. She looked thoughtful. When she spoke, her voice was calm. "We go to the food bank because sometimes there's not enough food for the whole month," she said. "And my dad's going to work as soon as he finds a new job. That's all!" She reached over to the first boy who had spoken and tapped him on the arm, "You're it!" They ran off in a whirl of squeals and laughter.

I walked back to the senior section of the playground, my heart flipping like a fish on a dock. That was cool the way Kayla could say what was in her mind without worrying about what other people would think.

I heard a familiar hearty laugh. Parker was in the vicinity. Maybe I should talk to him. Now that the gossip had been squelched, I wasn't feeling quite so mad at him. I scanned the blacktop but didn't see any sign of my large and boisterous friend. On the edge of the grass I caught sight of his trademark lime-green hoodie, heading toward the trees, beside some girl with short red hair . . .

Elsa? Victoria's best friend? What was he doing walking with Elsa?

I imagined marching over and demanding an explanation. *What's the meaning of this?* I could shout. They'd make up some phony explanation that I'd have to pretend to believe. Now I knew why Parker thought I'd cheated. He'd gone over to the other side.

To my relief, the bell went. I turned to go inside, trying to ignore the fact that I just saw my best friend being all friendly with the best friend of the enemy.

17

Once again, I was spending Saturday morning at the food bank. But this time I was excused from my usual job of moving boxes. I was now responsible for important computer business.

While I untangled cables and checked manuals, Sam came into Henry's office. She took in the mess of wires and computer parts. "What do you really have to do, Jelly? And don't tell me that gooey stuff you made up for Henry."

"Oh, hook up a computer, move the old data into a new program and set it up so your mom can type instead of having to write everything down," I said, with a nonchalant wave of my hand.

"I'm impressed."

Bonus.

I put together the components of the new computer and tested them. Piece of cake. Henry had given me a memory stick with the information from the old hard drive. I put it into the new computer, asked it nicely to import the data and watched in surprise, disbelief and growing horror as it politely told me that the memory stick was unreadable. *Format problems*, it said. *Corrupt file*, it suggested.

I took the memory stick home and scoured the Internet. Finding a clue online was a piece of something, but it wasn't cake. What I did find was that the old food bank computer program was beyond ancient. It probably used to compute on an abacus and print in Egyptian hieroglyphics. There were no current programs that would decode the memory stick. But Henry trusted me with this important thing, and I told him I would fix it. I couldn't let him down.

* * * * *

For the rest of the weekend, I searched for a hint that could help me understand the code. I was beginning to think Henry should not have had faith in me after all, when I came across an obscure reference in a long-dead thread of web conversation. There was someone who'd been working on the same problem and thought she'd found a solution.

I crossed my fingers and downloaded the conversion tool. My computer hummed as the bar millimetred its way to 100% complete, and I settled down in Dad's recliner for some well-deserved rest.

What a crazy life. I thought about my new friends. I felt I could talk to Henry about anything and he'd understand, even though he was much older than me. I wished I could be brave like Kayla. Then I thought about the speech contest and smiled. Victoria tried to ruin my chances but when Mrs. Muddgrove announced the winners on Monday morning, maybe my name would be the one she called.

I closed my eyes and dreamed I was holding a golden game controller high in the air while Victoria bowed her head before me. A crowd chanted my name. Then everything in my dream turned black. The controller burst into flames but I couldn't let go. It blazed in the dark while voices cried, "Cheater, cheater, cheater." The flames flashed toward my hand.

Heart thumping, I shuddered awake to the smell of smoke. Not the nice kind of smoke that comes from grilled meat or crackling logs. Nope, this was a nasty sort of plastic and electricity fog that hung in the air above the computer. I shot out of the recliner, pulled the plug and waved my hands. The flapping blew the haze around the basement and I gagged. What was going on? The computer screen stared blackly at me.

I called upstairs to Dad. He'd know what to do. He fixed this kind of thing all the time at work.

"What's wrong?" he asked. "Is the computer frozen again?"

"The opposite, Dad. It's fried."

He said, "Hmmmph," and came clomping down the stairs. When he saw the smoke, he gasped. "What did you do, Jelly?"

"Nothing. I was just downloading a program."

"What kind of program? You know you have to be careful about what you download from the Internet."

"It was an approved website, Dad. I made sure the anti-virus program said it was okay."

Dad sighed. "Well, it's a pretty old computer. I knew we'd need a replacement sometime."

"But I have to get this project done for the food bank."

Dad frowned and shook his head. "Sorry, Jelly. We can't afford a new computer right now. I'll take this one in to work on Monday and see what I can salvage."

I knew what *that* meant. It would take at least a week for Dad to run tests and diagnostics on his lunch hour. And then, from the smell of things, he wouldn't be able to fix it anyway.

"Well, maybe you can use your time to help your mom and me clean out the storage room in the basement instead."

"Dad! I don't have time for that. Henry's counting on me."

"Why can't you use the computer at the food bank?"

"There's no Internet there."

Dad looked surprised. "Well, maybe you could use Parker's computer."

"Yeah," I said. "I guess I could." But I honestly didn't feel like talking to Parker.

Dad's eyebrows creased like he was doing four-digit multiplication in his head. To my complete astonishment, he said, "I suppose, if you're in a serious bind, you *could* use my laptop."

18

On Monday, there was a big assembly in the gym to announce the winners of the first round of the speech competition. I sat with my class and tried to ignore Parker sitting beside Elsa. I also tried to ignore the shoulders and legs pressed against mine. No matter how small I made myself, I still touched someone else's clammy body part.

I looked around at the scoreboard with *Merry Men* printed above the *Home* sign, and the bits of paper and streamers stuck to the wall — remnants of past celebrations. Here's where we came when the weather was bad, to play King John jousting or Quarterstaff soccer.

It was so juvenile. This was the place where our teachers announced school stuff, but not the important things like your best friend has a girlfriend. Parker was so busy staring at Elsa, he didn't notice me staring at him.

Before we could find out who won the speech competition, we had to sit through a song about pumpkins by the kindergartens, complete with big actions and a little nose picking. Then the grade two teachers handed out ribbons to all their students for great spelling. The kid beside me said, "How could every one of them be so great at spelling?" Then Sam and the hip hop club did a dance demonstration.

Sam looked different up on stage with her ponytail tucked into a baseball cap. She wore baggy camouflage pants that ended below her knees and a tight-fitting tank top. Anyone wearing that tank top to class would've been sent home to change. I guessed the school dress code didn't extend to stage wear. All the other girls on stage wore the same outfits but I couldn't stop looking at Sam.

Whoa. Hang on! Sam was my best friend's sister. I liked hanging out with her and everything, but I didn't like her *that* way. At least, I didn't think I did. I watched the kid beside me. He seemed bored. I tried to look bored too. When the dancers strutted off the stage, they got a big round of applause. I clapped loudly for Sam.

The lights dimmed and a spotlight came on. The legendary tablet and all its gleaming accessories were carried onstage by the vice principal. He set them on a table near the podium. The spotlight swung over and lit them up. Mrs. Muddgrove walked across the stage, one hand in the air for silence. She held a piece of paper in her other hand. The noisy chatter died away. We shifted our behinds on the cold, hard floor and waited. Mrs. Muddgrove shook the sheet of paper and peered at it. She picked up her tiny glasses from where they hung at her chest and put them on her nose. She peered at the paper again and cleared her throat.

"As you know," she said, "the winners of the first round of the speech competition are chosen by a vote of their peers."

I crossed my fingers.

"We have had something of a dilemma in one of the classes," Mrs. Muddgrove continued. "The votes were split exactly in half between two competitors. After much discussion, the administration has decided to allow both students to move on to the second phase of the competition." A murmur went through the gym.

I wasn't paying much attention to Mrs. Muddgrove's babbling. I was busy crossing and recrossing my fingers and trying to cross my toes at the ends of my crossed legs. I sweated as she went through the list of names.

When she read out, "Victoria Viscount," I felt a stab of disappointment, and a flood of relief that I wouldn't have to give my speech again. Victoria flashed me a look of triumph. So when Mrs. Muddgrove said, "Joe Miles," I thought she'd made a mistake. But someone shook me by the shoulders, and that's when I realized I was still in the running against Victoria — and about eight other winning speeches. This time, pride and fear washed over me.

The principal held up her hand again as we fidgeted and looked toward the exits.

"The final competition will be held in two weeks. However . . ." and here she waited until all eyes were on her. "*This* year, in light of the substantial prize that will be awarded, we have decided to add another challenge." She paused again to let that little nugget of information sink in.

Challenge? What kind of challenge? You had to give your speech underwater? Eat worms? Find your way out of a maze while reciting the thing? What?

"The competitors must prepare and present a second speech for the finals. The topic must be entirely different from their first."

A whole new speech?

It was a miracle I'd come up with even one.

* * * * *

At lunchtime, I saw Sam standing at Parker's locker. I ignored Parker and said to Sam, "Your hip hop club looked good up there." I couldn't help noticing how blue her eyes looked with her dance makeup still on. It gave me a funny feeling in my chest.

She smiled and said, "Thanks. Congrats on getting into the finals, Jelly."

"Yeah, that's huge, dude," said Parker. "But I'm bummed. The demise of rock 'n' roll got beat out by some speech on hairstyles."

"At least mine lost to a worthy topic," said Sam.

Parker said, "Ha, I can't believe that someone in your class talked about what they'd do about global warming if they were prime minister."

"You'll be glad she gave it so much thought when she *is* prime minister," said Sam.

Parker turned serious. "Hey, I'm sorry I doubted you, Jelly."

"That's okay," I heard myself saying. But I didn't feel okay.

"Did you hear about Victoria?" asked Sam.

That got our full attention. Sam said that after the assembly, she'd followed Victoria and a bunch of her friends. They marched to the office and protested the new contest rules. "Victoria said there was lack of consistency and fairness," said Sam. "She told Mrs. Muddgrove that

Jelly shouldn't be allowed to compete because his topic was frivolous and possibly copied."

"What did Muddgrove say?" asked Parker.

"She looked mad when Victoria said 'copied.' She told Victoria if she didn't think she could handle the competition, she could always step down."

We laughed.

19

It felt good to share a laugh with Parker. After school, we got on the bus, just like old times. I wanted to ask him about Elsa and why he'd stuck up for Victoria when I said she was mean. Instead, we went to his house with Spencer and played Rebel Ruckus. Spencer and Parker tried to think of a new speech topic for me: why people should eat more junk food; how to cheat at Scrabble; or the top five reasons why you don't need to brush your teeth every day.

None of them felt right.

Being around Parker didn't feel right.

The next day, back at school, even though it was a sunny day, my thoughts were dark. What was going on between Parker and Elsa? How on earth was I going to figure out the computer program for the food bank? When would I have time to come up with a new speech, much less write one?

It was hot at recess and I got permission from the teacher on duty to get a drink of water from inside. As I walked by the student council office, I heard Parker's rumbly voice. I peeked in the doorway and saw him sitting at the big work table, his back to me. Beside him, a red-haired girl bent her head toward him. Parker's arm was around the back of her chair and he pointed at something on the table.

Startled, I stepped back from the door.

A voice behind me said, "Y'know, now that you've done those projects for student council, we don't need you anymore."

Victoria stood behind me with, no surprise, Becky. Victoria had a satisfied look on her face. "I guess you *didn't* know," she said. "Your so-called friend's been making goo-goo eyes at Elsa since school started." She giggled. "P.B. wanted to impress her so much, he said he'd make the posters for student council." She snorted. "He can't draw worth beans, so he conned *you* into doing them."

Realization dawned on me. I'd been duped, fooled. But how could that be? Parker was my best friend.

Was!

Parker must have heard the talking. He came outside, followed by Elsa. He glanced from Victoria and Becky to me, frowning.

I couldn't keep it in. "I can't believe you tricked me like that!"

"Like what?" he asked. "What are you talking about?"

"You! You got me to help you because you couldn't make the posters yourself. You made me do them so Elsa would like you."

"Hey, that's so not true," said Parker.

"You wouldn't know what's true." I practically spit the words. "You thought I cheated on my speech."

"Jelly, you have no idea . . ." said Elsa.

Victoria started to laugh.

Shaking, I strode away. I didn't want to hear anything anyone had to say.

No one came after me this time, and that suited me fine.

20

For the rest of the week, I sat next to Spencer on the bus and walked straight home.

I borrowed Dad's laptop and held my breath while I downloaded the conversion program. The laptop didn't go up in smoke, so that was a good start. I stayed up late checking user groups and searching online manuals to help me fine-tune the program. It was more complicated than I'd thought, but I didn't want to let Henry down.

Henry called me every afternoon for an update. That was okay at first when I needed to know the kinds of numbers and graphs he wanted. After that I didn't have anything to report. But he still kept calling.

Mom and Dad didn't bug me about staying up past my

bedtime. Dad came down one night and sat in the chair beside me. "Your mom and I are happy that you're working so hard for the food bank," he said.

"Thanks."

"I guess all the hours you spend making games on the computer isn't a *complete* waste of time." He smiled at the look on my face. "We know you're not just doing homework down here." He leaned over and ruffled my hair. "That speech you wrote about gaming was pretty good too."

My heart leaped. "What if my next speech wins the prize?"

Dad looked at the ceiling and pursed his lips. "Screen things are a distraction from more important things. Don't get your hopes up, Jelly."

* * * * *

By the end of the week I was exhausted. In the mirror, I saw dark circles under my red eyes. And I fell asleep during a movie in science.

On Saturday morning, Mom kissed the top of my head where it rested on the table and said, "Sweetie, you look pale. Eat something."

Eating seemed like too much effort. I drank a glass of milk and grabbed the memory stick before getting into Mrs. Brown's car. Sam chattered all the way, making up for P.B. being away at hockey yet again. By the time we arrived at the food bank I had a headache and a bellyache.

Sam and her mom went to the main room, while I headed to Henry's office and booted up the new computer. I loaded the program I'd modified and popped the memory stick into the drive. I clicked on the *run* and then the *save* icons. I crossed my fingers and waited for the data to convert.

In a flash, there were error messages all over the screen. All that work — useless. I'd have to go over my notes to find out what went wrong. *Okay, fine,* I thought. *It's just a matter of time before I figure it out.* But when I checked the memory stick, I found that the program had saved the defective data *over* the original information. And in spite of all my frantic efforts, I couldn't get it to undo or go back. Years of information — gone. And I hadn't made a backup!

Henry poked his head in the door and asked, "So, champ, how's it going?"

"Not so good," I muttered.

"Are you close to being done?"

"Um, not really."

"What's taking so long?"

I felt sick. How could I tell him I'd just lost the years and years of data he'd collected? "Things aren't going exactly how I planned."

His eyes narrowed. "I hope you're not goofing off. Those numbers have to be ready in time for my presentation."

Goofing off?

"Well," I said, "maybe if *you'd* got a start on it, it'd be finished by now."

Henry flinched. I felt bad, but I wanted him to go away and leave me in peace.

He didn't go away. He set his hands on his hips and leaned over so the light bounced off his shaved head. In a low voice he said, "You're gonna have to work harder, Jelly."

Suddenly, besides the terrible guilty feeling I had in my stomach, I also felt furious. It's one thing to have people get mad at you when you do something wrong. But I was trying to bail him out with his stupid computer and things had gone horribly wrong. This was a very bad time to be snarling at me.

"Forget it!" I said, pushing the chair away from the desk. "I can't do this anymore." My head throbbed. I got up and went to the front desk. "Can I use the phone, please, Mrs. Brown?"

"Sure, Jelly, what's the matter?"

"I'm going to call my mom to pick me up. I have to go home."

Then I remembered. Mom and Dad were out all morning. I stood there, my hand hovering over the phone.

Mrs. Brown's eyes flicked over to Henry standing by his office door. "No need to call your mom," she said. "I'll take you."

I couldn't speak. I stared at the desk and nodded.

We drove in silence. I looked out the window so Mrs. Brown wouldn't see my face. When we got home I mumbled, "Thanks," and let myself in with my key. I went up to my room and lay on the bed. My head and stomach still hurt but now something else ached, right in the middle of my chest.

* * * * *

After a while, the doorbell rang. I snuck a look out my bedroom window. It was Mrs. Brown and Henry standing on the front porch. I pulled my head back and waited. But the doorbell rang again. And again. I dragged myself downstairs and opened the door. Henry really was big. The snake tattoo and earring seemed more threatening than usual. I was glad Mrs. Brown was there.

"Henry told me what happened, Jelly," she said. "Will you come outside so we can talk?"

I stepped out on the porch, and Henry thrust a paper bag into my hands. "Payment for last week's work," he muttered. "You took off before I could give it to you." I peered inside — a cardboard cup of hot chocolate, cold by now I bet, and two jelly doughnuts.

"I'm not hun—" I began. But when my stomach growled, I reached in for a doughnut. After I'd eaten two bites, I realized I was famished.

I devoured the rest and washed it back with a mouthful of warmish chocolate. I didn't feel sick in my stomach anymore and my headache was disappearing. But I still had that hard hurt in the middle of my chest.

Henry watched me with a worried look. He cleared his throat. "Jelly, I was a real jerk back there. I'm sorry I said those things to you."

I felt relieved and miserable. "That's okay," I said. "I was pretty rude to you, Henry."

"No, it's not okay. I should know better than to take out my frustrations on you. I'll stick to what I know and let you do your job."

I tried to keep the quaver out of my voice. "I can't. I totally messed up and I don't know what to do."

Henry and Mrs. Brown stared at me.

"I lost all the numbers on the memory stick." I blinked hard.

"Oh my," said Mrs. Brown. "Is that very bad?"

Henry frowned and stuck out his chin. "You wrecked the memory stick?" He spread his meaty hands wide and grinned. "No big deal. I've got a bunch of backup copies in my desk."

I'm sure my eyes bugged out.

I resisted the urge to hug him. My breath shuddered, and I said, as calmly as I could, "That . . . that's a relief."

"I learned one thing in computer class. Make lots of copies of the important stuff." He held out his hand. "Are we okay, now?"

I shook his hand enthusiastically.

Henry took a deep breath. "I guess I should explain to both of you why everything went so badly with me and the computer."

Mrs. Brown looked puzzled.

"I went to the computer classes," said Henry, "but I had trouble reading the textbooks and taking notes. I thought I'd be able to figure it out by watching what the instructor did on her computer. But it all started to go too fast for me to keep up, and I got completely lost at the end."

"You can't read?" I blurted out.

Henry turned red. I felt bad for saying it out loud.

"Well, I *can* read," he said. "Easy things, at least. But not those textbooks. I get dizzy just looking at them."

Henry squinted at the ground, shifting from one foot to the other. He suddenly seemed tiny standing there in front of Mrs. Brown.

"Oh, Henry, that explains some things," she said.

"I know I should've been doing the books and inventory myself, Rose. But I got this far without having to do a lot of reading and writing, and I was too embarrassed to tell anyone why I couldn't do the computer part."

Mrs. Brown put her hand on his arm. "Don't be so hard on yourself, Henry. Nobody's perfect." She patted him. "It'll be okay," she said. "And I'm sure Jelly will get this done in time." She looked at me uncertainly.

"When *is* your deadline?" I said. Why had I not asked this before?

"I need the numbers in a week," replied Henry.

"No probs." I smiled bravely at the two grown-ups. "It'll be done by then."

21

I barely heard Mr. Chan tell the class about our new computer assignment. It was a project to build a class website, something I'd normally think was fun and super easy, if I weren't so sleep deprived. He paired us up — boys with girls. I got Elsa for a partner. She pulled her chair over to my computer and glanced at Victoria, who sat at the far end of the class with Jeff. Poor Jeff.

I busied myself reading the sheet Mr. Chan had given us. I turned to Elsa and found her staring at me. "Um," I said. "It says we should start by —"

She interrupted me with a whisper, "Victoria's a liar."

I frowned at her, confused.

"She told me she heard you bragging that you stole that speech."

What?

"And I told P.B." She twisted her pencil in her hands. "I'm sorry, Jelly, but I believed her. And P.B. believed me."

I thought about that for a moment. "What about P.B. getting me to do things for council?" I whispered back.

"P.B. asked you to help because you're his friend and he knew you'd do a great job."

"And you weren't sticking around with P.B. so you could get information on me for Victoria?"

Elsa looked shocked. "Man, are you paranoid. I *like* P.B.," she said. "Besides, ever since Victoria tried to get you in trouble for pushing her, I haven't even talked to her." Elsa pointed her pencil at me. "She's trying to make you think P.B.'s against you. But that's not true. He's always been your friend."

"Then why didn't he stick up for me when the rumours were going around?"

"Why are *you* so quick to believe Victoria?" She sighed. "Do you honestly think that P.B.'s the kind of person who'd ditch his best friend?"

Good point.

Life's complicated.

* * * * *

I'd done programming at school and created games on my computer at home for fun. But converting the data for Henry wasn't for fun, and there weren't marks on the line. People were depending on me. When Ms Mitrovika excused Victoria and me from English so we could work on our speeches, I went to the library. Instead of doing research, I used the computer to sweat over the program for the food bank.

At home on Friday night, I finished the third program rewrite. I made several backups. It was down to the wire. If I didn't get this working now, Mrs. Brown wouldn't have enough time to enter the new data in time for Henry's presentation. With shaking hands, I plugged the memory stick into the drive. I waited for the laptop to give me the okay and I hit *convert* on the menu. This had to be the one. The program that would change ones and zeros into something a modern spreadsheet could understand. I held my breath as the converted file was imported into the new program. And I felt a thrill as I saw the empty cells fill up with names and numbers. I hugged Dad's laptop and danced with it around the room.

* * * * *

When we got to the food bank the next morning, Henry was unloading the truck. I waved the memory stick at him. "The program's ready to go."

He came over and said, "Great job, buddy." He smiled. "You need me to help you with anything?"

I shook my head. I could teach Henry about computers when this was all done. Right now, he was too busy. He'd already signed himself up for a literacy class at night.

I sat down at the big wooden desk in Henry's office and turned on the computer. I put the memory stick into the drive and selected the commands. It didn't take longer than a blink. Well, maybe two blinks. The cells on the spreadsheet filled up with food bank words, like Dad's laptop had.

I pulled Mrs. Brown into the office. "Ooh," she said, as she sat down, "I'm excited to try this out." I showed her how to click on each item and answer the questions that came up. "Oh my," she said, "it's so sophisticated." When the last screen winked off, she gazed at me in wonder. "You're brilliant, Jelly. It won't take me any time to type in the rest."

I felt my cheeks get hot. The program wasn't all that fancy compared to some of the stuff I'd seen on the Internet. But, I suppose, to adults who'd only played Atari, it would seem like something out of *Star Wars*.

Mrs. Brown ran outside and got Henry. She sat him down in front of the computer. Henry shifted in the chair. "I'm not sure . . ."

"Yes, you can," said Mrs. Brown. "Jelly made it so simple, even we of the more mature generation can do it."

I wondered how much Henry could read. Would he be embarrassed if he didn't know what was on the screen? I knew I would be. I watched as the menu came up. Henry ran his finger down the monitor to the words in each of the boxes I'd created: *New Family, Existing Family, Summary* and *Exit*. He moved the cursor to *New Family* and clicked. I watched as he read each line: *Last Name, First Name, Names of Family Members* . . . Mrs. Brown helped him with the word *Relationship*.

When he got to the last screen, Henry shook his head. "Nice work, kid. Even an old fogey like me can figure this out."

He was even more impressed when he saw the slide-show presentation of charts and graphs. Colourful bars and lines showed how many families used the food bank and which were the busiest days of the year.

"Wow!" said Henry. "These will explain what we do here better than I can."

I tried to look humble and pleased at the same time.

"Good for you, Jelly." The sound of that voice set the hairs on the back of my neck on end. Victoria stood at the doorway with her arms folded.

Henry smacked me on the back and grinned. "Yeah, he's amazing, ain't he?"

Victoria?

Mrs. Brown turned away from the computer. "Oh, Jelly, I think you know our new volunteer."

Victoria smiled. "Hi, Mrs. Brown. Hi, Henry." Her voice was all aspartame. That fake sweetness might fool some grown-ups, but I knew better.

"What are *you* doing here?" I asked.

"Oh, I thought I'd spend some time . . ." She pursed her lips. "You know, helping the less fortunate." She gave me a smile that didn't reach her eyes, and then walked over to where Sam sorted tins.

"Your friend's been coming after school every day this week," Henry said. "She's a big help." He leaned over and said out of the side of his mouth, "But bossy."

I didn't get it. Why would Victoria show up at the food bank? Maybe it wasn't enough for her to cause me grief all week at school; maybe she'd decided to carry on her reign of terror after hours.

Elsa was right. I was paranoid.

"I gotta finish unloading the truck. Nice work, Jelly," said Henry, as he hustled out the door.

Mrs. Brown patted my shoulder. "Well done," she said. "I'm going to get the books and start putting the numbers in the computer. Why don't you give Sam and Victoria a hand? We're awfully busy."

I left her with the computer and went to find Sam so I could tell her, modestly, that my program rocked.

"So," asked Victoria, "have you been practising for the competition?"

Earlier in the week, I'd thought about my upcoming speech. But seeing as I hadn't written it, I hadn't done any practising.

"It'll be so much better than the first one," she said, rubbing her hands together. "There'll be oodles of people watching."

The thought of oodles of people watching gave me the shivers, and once again, I could think of nothing particularly witty to say.

For the past two weeks, I'd been researching computer scripting programs and writing code. I'd ignored everything to do with school. Now I had to give a speech in two days.

Two days!

And, it couldn't just be good. If I wanted to beat Victoria — and I did — it had to be stupendous!

22

Once Sam and her mom dropped me off at home, I calculated I had exactly one-and-a-half whole days to prepare for the speech competition.

I hadn't meant to leave it so late and I felt panicky. I imagined getting up in front of the entire gym filled with students and their parents, and actual judges, judging me. Nobody would be surprised if I picked a random topic, read my notes as fast as I could and then stepped away from the podium. I could see Victoria with her superior smile, saying, "Good try, Jelly," as she won first place.

I was getting tired of Victoria thinking she could intimidate me into giving up. It was hard enough to present a speech, but I knew I could do it. I just needed a kick-butt topic. The more I thought about it, the more my mind felt like an empty chalkboard.

Desperately, I searched my room for inspiration. I scanned my bookshelf. Who'd want to hear about how to translate Elvish into English? There were drawings on the wall of Leonardo and Michelangelo that I'd made when I was younger. Would anyone care which Renaissance artists the Ninja Turtles were named for?

I sat down at my desk. Sticking out from a pile of gaming magazines was a colourful bit of paper. I pulled it out. It was my class picture from last year. Parker and Sam were in it. I knew what Parker would tell me to write about. How about Sam? She'd want me to talk about getting involved. What did I know about that? All I was involved with was video games and computers . . . and the food bank.

Hey! Now that could make a prize-winning speech.

I made a list:

• food banks give food to people who need it (well, *duh*)

• all sorts of people use food banks, even kids like me (*double-duh* — though I guess I didn't know that at first)

• being hungry can make you feel sick and cranky and dizzy (like giving a speech)

• helping others makes you feel good (as good as beating the boss in Rebel Ruckus)

I wanted it to be interesting — not filled with boring numbers and facts — so I wrote about what I'd expected when I first went to Food Share and what I thought now. Only I wrote it as if some other kid had the experience. I didn't want anyone to think I used to be prejudiced about the food bank. I typed it up on Dad's laptop and organized it so it made sense. Then I fell asleep at the desk. I woke up in the middle of the night with a crick in my neck and drool on my cheek. I turned off the light and hauled myself to bed.

* * * * *

The next morning I walked over to Parker's house. I remembered when Sundays meant hanging out with my friends and procrastinating doing homework till the afternoon. I wasn't sure what I was going to say to Parker. His mom let me in and told me he was in the basement with Spencer. I felt a little prickle of nerves as I went downstairs. But when Parker came roaring at me and wrestled me to the ground, I knew everything would be all right.

Spencer was pleased to see me too. "We couldn't play Ruckus with only two," he said. "Sam told us you're helping out at the food bank."

"That's all she ever talks about." Parker smiled sweetly and batted his eyelashes at me.

"Did she tell you Victoria's volunteering at the food bank too?"

"Yeah. That's so weird," said Parker.

"C'mon, Jelly," said Spencer. "Grab a controller. Let's play."

"I can't. I want you guys to tell me what you think about my new speech."

"Okay," said Spencer reluctantly. "Speech us."

I suddenly felt self-conscious but I read from my notes, "Every day, many people are hungry for lots of different reasons. The food bank is there to help."

I told them what my imaginary kid had done at the food bank, what he'd learned, how he'd changed. I made my last point and looked at my friends. Their eyes were glazed over. Parker pretended to startle himself awake with a sleepy wheeze. I didn't feel offended. I would've done the same.

"So?" I asked.

"It sounds like you copied it from the newspaper," said Spencer. He added, "That's not a compliment."

"Dude, I hate to say this," said Parker. "Like, it didn't sound like you."

"What d'ya mean? I wrote it."

But I understood what he meant. I was trying to write a speech like Victoria's. Unfortunately, I couldn't act passionate about it like she did. I cared about the food bank, but I'd never be able to get other people excited about it.

"You know that first speech you gave?" said Parker. "It

was good because you wrote it like you told me to write my speech — from the heart." He thumped his chest and broke into a Tarzan yell.

"It was funny too," added Spencer. "That was probably the best part."

"Yeah," I muttered. The problem was I didn't have any heart or funny left.

Mr. Brown shouted down that it was time for Parker's hockey practice, and I went home. At least I *had* a speech. I stopped to chat with Roger, all comfy in his chair. "I don't think my speech is good enough," I said.

He stared back at me, silent.

In my room, I examined my notes. Maybe I could do a better speech. But only if I were the kind of person who could go on stage in front of a zillion people and not care if he made a complete jackass of himself. I imagined myself giving the speech I wished I could write. The kind I'd want to hear.

And I finally realized that it wasn't Victoria who prevented me from giving that speech. It was me, for believing her when she made fun of me, for letting her tell me who I was. I sat down for a while and thought, not about speeches, but about the kind of person I wanted to be. It was time for a fresh start.

I went downstairs and called, "Hey, Dad, can I ask you a favour?"

23

It was speech day, and I didn't hear a single word in my classes. I felt a constant jangle of fear-excitement inside. Whenever there was a break, I pulled the notes from my back pocket and reread them. I imagined where I'd do gestures and where I'd pause. At the end of the day, it was memorized. I raced home and practised some more. I managed two bites of dinner, something called spaghetti squash that looked, but didn't taste anything like noodles. "Dad," I asked. "When you used to work in front of a crowd, did you ever get stage fright?"

"You bet," he said. "But after a while I realized that the audience was on my side. They just wanted to be entertained."

I nodded. That's how I felt when I listened to other people's presentations.

After dinner, I collected my backpack and met my parents waiting by the door. Mom gave me a big hug. "I am so proud of you," she said.

"I haven't even given my speech yet."

"It doesn't matter what your speech is like. You're doing something very brave. And you should know . . ."

"You should know that if you *do* win," said Dad, "I'll be the first to take you on at Battle MegaZed."

I rolled my eyes, then gave him a high-five.

"What's in the backpack?" asked Mom.

"It's—"

Dad put a finger to his lips. "A surprise, Gracie."

I rode in the back seat with our neighbour, Mr. Whitaker. He lives alone and loves coming to these things. He calls it having a night out.

There were lots of cars in the school parking lot, and the gym was humming. Chairs were set out in tight rows. Someone had removed the scraps of paper that were usually stuck to the walls. The gym lights felt blindingly bright, and the dark green walls had taken on an eerie sheen. People filed in and jostled for seats at the front or on the aisles. It seemed as if most of the students, and a lot of parents, had turned out to cheer on their friends and family.

I saw Sam and Parker come in with Mr. and Mrs. Brown, and Elsa and Spencer. I was walking over to say hello when a heavy hand gripped my shoulder and a huge voice boomed, "Hey, Jelly."

"Hey, Henry," I said. "What're you doing here?"

"I came to see you give your winning speech."

Mom and Dad came over and I introduced them to Henry. I didn't feel like making chit-chat, so I shouldered my backpack and left to find Ms Mitrovika.

I looked around when I heard Victoria's voice. She'd arrived with her parents, her shiny black shoes tap-tapping on the wooden floor. She wore a frilly dress, and her hair was pulled into a mound of stiff curls on the top of her head.

I watched as her dad made a bunch of people move over so he could sit where he would get the best shot with his video camera. Her mom made a big show of fixing something in Victoria's hair, even though Victoria tried to wave her off. Then her mom went searching for a teacher, saying loudly, "How are we supposed to know where the competitors sit? There should be someone directing traffic here." Victoria stood by her dad while he fiddled with his camera. Becky went over and Victoria perked up, showing off her outfit.

As I walked past the stage, I noticed the old wooden podium that the principal used when she lectured us about being respectful to substitute teachers. For tonight's festivities, someone had draped it in silver fabric and grey ribbon. It looked sharp and glittery. Clipped to the edge of the lectern was a large black microphone. Nearby, on a little table, was the tablet surrounded by the newest keyboard, the fancy stylus, the game controller. Even without the spotlight, they seemed to glow ominously from within.

I finally found Ms Mitrovika and she said, "Contestants sit in the front row, of course. Those seats are reserved just for you." She smiled as if I should feel pleased about that.

I had to sit beside Victoria. Though I was on a chair instead of the hard floor, it was very uncomfortable. I felt as if everyone was staring at the back of my head, but I didn't look around in case it was true. I took slow breaths and tried to keep the fear-excitement gathered into a small, cold knot in my middle, instead of rampaging through my whole body.

At seven o'clock sharp, Ms Mitrovika went onstage and introduced the judges: Mrs. Muddgrove, Ms Longo the librarian and Mr. Spears the bigwig school board superintendent. They sat on the side of the stage so the contestants couldn't see them but could feel the critical eyes boring into the sides of their heads.

The evening started with the youngest grades. It was no consolation being last again.

Darla told us why a kangaroo would make a good pet. Robbie talked about his grandfather the inventor. There were speeches about hockey legends, clothing styles through the ages and uses for old cutlery. Their words were like a dull roar in my head. All I could think of was how strange it was that my heart beat so hard but no one seemed to hear it.

Victoria sat cool and collected beside me and occasionally snickered when someone flubbed their lines. Every now and then she sneaked a sideways peek at me. I kept my eyes on the stage and tried not to think of the moment when I would make a complete fool of myself in front of all these people.

When her turn came, Victoria stood and shook out the folds of her fluffy dress. She tapped up the steps, onto the stage and over to the podium. She smiled into the audience. The lights dimmed as the first slide appeared on a large white screen behind Victoria, a close-up of her standing in front of a hazy brown building.

"Good evening, ladies and gentlemen, boys and girls," she began. "Tonight, I'm going to tell you about an invisible group that lives and works beside us in our community."

Invisible group? Ghosts? No way. Victoria would never choose a topic as trivial as the paranormal.

Victoria continued, "Tonight, I am going to tell you about the people who frequent the food bank."

So *that's* why she'd been at Food Share. I tried to concentrate as she expounded on the fine qualities of the food bank. She talked about the people who went there and the generous givers from the community. She made it sound like she'd volunteered there forever and, thanks to her, there was always enough for everyone. She even used statistics about how many tonnes of food were distributed each year and how many families were helped.

At the end, Victoria, who had not let Sam start a fundraiser for Food Share, promised that as head of student council she would arrange a food drive so amazing that it would probably end world hunger. I glanced at the judges' table and caught Mrs. Muddgrove dabbing a tissue at her eyes. Yup, Victoria had done it again. She'd given a perfect speech for the judges — full of impressive numbers, passionate and moving.

The lights came back up as Victoria tossed her head and descended the steps to her parents' wild applause. She sat down and honoured me with a self-satisfied smirk.

"Take that, loser," she whispered.

Right then, I could barely hear her over the rushing of blood in my ears. I couldn't get enough oxygen, and no matter how often I wiped my hands on my jeans, my palms felt like Niagara Falls. But that last little dig was the shove I needed to get onstage. Victoria thought only about winning. I had the crazy idea that she'd volunteered at Food Share so she could find out my speech topic and do it first. Then the judges would think I was a copycat. But my speech wasn't written for a bunch of judges. I wrote my speech for me — me and the audience.

The judges took a minute to tabulate the score for Victoria. A whole excruciating sixty seconds while I told myself that I didn't want the silly prize anyway. I could back down and concede defeat.

Yeah, right. Victoria would never let me live that down.

Finally, Ms Mitrovika introduced me and waved me up. I picked up my backpack, feeling light-headed as I stood. I forced my feet to the stage and turned around.

This was going to be the scariest thing I'd ever done in my whole life. I looked down into the expanse of gleaming eyes and willed myself to focus on the next step ahead. I just had to make it through the next five minutes, word by word.

Then it would be over.

24

Sam stood out in the crowd. She wore a bright orange dress and had tossed a purple scarf around her shoulders. She sat very still, hands clasped in her lap. Parker was beside her, his two thumbs up. Henry leaned across my parents to say something to Mr. Whitaker. My parents looked excited and nervous.

In a moment the overhead lights would dim and I'd be blinded by the spotlight. That would be good. Dad had told me his secret to overcoming stage fright. It was to pretend that everyone in the audience was a stranger and he'd never have to see them again.

I peeked into my backpack and checked on Roger. Besides my parents and Parker, I've known him all my life and he's always been there for me. Roger looked back and, I swear, he winked.

The lights in the gym flicked out and the spotlight flashed on. I could no longer see the crowd. I kept the image of Parker and his two thumbs up in my head; everyone else became a fuzzy stranger. There was a murmur when I reached into the backpack and pulled out Roger. I settled him on the lectern, beside the microphone. With trembling hands, I leaned him into the mike and he said, "Testing," in his squeaky voice. I made him tap it with his forehead. "Testing. Is this thing on?" A ripple of amusement ran through the gym.

I turned Roger's head to scan the audience and he opened his mouth. "Good evening, ladies and gentlemen. My name is Roger and I'd like to introduce my assistant, Joe Miles." I smiled tentatively into the darkness as Roger said, "Say hello to the nice people, Joe."

It was so much easier to speak for Roger than myself, but I said, "Hello," and bobbed my head.

Voices said, "Hello," back.

"Tonight," said Roger, "Joe will have the pleasant task of standing with his hand up my — *ahem* — behind while I make fun of him."

I glared at him while the audience chuckled.

He turned to me, and my fingers on the control stick made his eyes go wide. "Whoa, Joe. Just kidding — I won't make fun of you." I turned him back to the audience. "Tonight Joe will enlighten us on the finer points of how to give a speech."

I mimed reaching into my front pocket. I patted my sides and rear pockets. I made a despairing face at Roger.

"You forgot your cue cards?" He made a large sigh and rolled his eyes. "You dummy."

The audience gasped and chortled.

"The first thing to remember when making a speech," said Roger, "is to bring your notes."

I shrugged, pulling my shoulders all the way up to my ears. Then I slouched awkwardly against the lectern, spare hand in my pocket.

"The next thing is to maintain correct posture." Roger turned and stared pointedly at me. I straightened up quickly. "Try to act natural," he said.

"I am acting natural," I retorted.

Roger raised his eyebrows. "You seem a little wooden to me."

While the gym rang with laughter, I turned and squinted at the wall.

Roger continued, "It's important to maintain eye contact with your audience." As I gazed into space, he leaned over and smacked the side of my head. There was a fresh wave of laughter. I jumped to attention, faced the crowd and muttered some gibberish.

"Speak loudly and clearly. Don't mumble," said Roger, sternly.

I turned to the mike and ran my words together. "I-know-don't-talk-too-fast-or-no-one-will-understand-you," I said. Then I forced myself to slow down to half speed. "But . . . don't . . . talk . . . too . . . slowly . . . either . . . or . . . you'll . . . lose . . ."

Roger closed his eyes, and his head rolled to one side. He let out a gentle snore. I could hear Parker's guffaws above the laughter in the crowd. Roger opened one eye and shook his head at me.

I exhaled and we carried on.

Roger introduced the rules and I did the opposite.

Each time, the audience roared its approval.

Finally, "When making a speech," Roger said, "avoid saying the same thing twice."

I pushed him away from the mike and said, "Try not to repeat yourself."

Roger muscled in front of me. "Don't be redundant."

"Don't say stuff over and over," I countered.

Before Roger could reply, I shouted, "*In short, you shouldn't rephrase, restate or reiterate!*" I stood back and smiled smugly.

Roger turned to me and waited. Gradually it became quiet. He gazed into the hushed gym, first to the left then to the right. He leaned into the microphone, opened his mouth and said . . . "Ditto."

I picked Roger up from the lectern and put him on my arm. Together we turned to the darkened hall and took a deep bow — to a storm of cheers and whistles.

I dared to look at the judges' table. In the dim light I saw the superintendent leaning back in his chair, tears of laughter running down his face.

25

The lights in the gym came back on and I blinked. Parker was on his feet, grinning his crazy clown grin, shouting, *"Yeah, Jelly!"* and punching the air with his fist. Sam stood beside him, laughing and clapping. Henry, Elsa and Spencer stood too. I heard the scrape of chairs as people rose to their feet, and the rumble of applause. Mom and Dad were smiling as if their faces would break. Old Mr. Whitaker sat and thumped on the floor with his cane. A quick glance at Victoria's face filled me with joy. A perfectly balanced mixture of confusion and fury. *Ni-ce!*

I put Roger in my backpack and stumbled down the stairs feeling as if I would burst. I didn't look at Victoria as I sat down. And from the way her body was turned stiffly away, I got the impression she didn't particularly want to see me either. The crowd chattered and shuffled as we waited for the judges to tally the scores and make their final decision. Now that it was over, I couldn't stop shaking. I concentrated on getting my arms and legs to stop jumping around and my heart rate back to normal.

When the judges were ready, Ms Mitrovika walked over to their table and took the sheet of paper Mrs. Mudd-grove held out. It didn't matter whether I won or lost, I told myself. It only mattered that I'd done my best and the audience enjoyed it.

I was such a liar.

The microphone buzzed and I held my breath. The lights dimmed once more, and Ms Mitrovika peered out into the dark. "On behalf of the contestants, staff and audience members," she said, "I wish to extend thanks to the judges who have generously given their time to be part of this special event and to carry out a task which, tonight, was quite difficult. Every speaker did a wonderful job."

The audience clapped.

"In a moment," Ms Mitrovika said, "I'll announce the three winners of the speech competition. Each will be awarded a medal of merit, and the first-place winner will be the proud owner of this tablet computer, generously donated by the Sinclair family."

She pointed at it gleaming quietly in the corner. At this rate I could suffocate before I found out who was going to take home the prize.

My prize.

Ms Mitrovika began, "The winners are, in no particular order..."

Beside me, I sensed Victoria preparing to rise.

"Trina Baker, Victoria Viscount and..."

Joe Miles, Joe Miles, Joe Miles, I repeated over and over in my head, willing her to say it.

"Joseph Miles," said Ms Mitrovika.

My heart skipped a beat.

Trina Baker jumped to her feet, ran up the stairs and wrapped her arms around Ms Mitrovika's waist. Victoria patted the curls at the side of her head, shook her skirt into place as she stood and swept up the stairs like royalty. I staggered up behind her and stood beside Trina, who bobbed up and down with excitement. Victoria shot her a withering glare but Trina paid no attention.

"Our third-place winner," announced Ms Mitrovika, "is Trina Baker for her speech on going green. Terrific work, Trina." Ms Mitrovika put the big bronze medal around Trina's neck and handed her a certificate. Trina smiled radiantly as she bounced on her toes.

"Both Victoria and Joseph gave outstanding speeches tonight. Victoria moved the judges with her heartfelt speech about the food bank, and Joseph entertained us with his useful advice on how to give a speech. The winner of this year's speech competition is . . ."

The pause felt like an hour, a day, a week. There was enough time to think about how, in a few short weeks, I'd taken on Victoria and found that I still lived. Maybe knowing that was worth more than having my own computer.

More lies.

Ms Mitrovika's voice faded away as I repeated *Joe Miles* in my head.

I heard the applause of the crowd. I watched Ms Mitrovika turn to Victoria and put the gold medal over her massive head of curls. Then she gave her a certificate and shook her hand. Victoria smiled down her nose at the audience and made a little curtsy. She turned her eyes on me and her mouth twitched up higher. My own lips quivered perilously downward but I forced a grimace.

I made my way to Ms Mitrovika on leaden feet, and she put a heavy silver medal around my neck. She handed me a piece of paper that said, *Speech Competition Winner, Second Place*. I stared into the gym. All the lights were blazing now. I saw my dad beaming as he clapped. My mom's eyes were shining. Sam waved her purple scarf over her head like a banner. Parker mouthed something but all I heard was a rush of white noise.

As soon as I got off the stage, everyone crowded around. Parker yelled, *"Way to go, Joe!"* Parents shook my hand. Mr. Whitaker shuffled over and growled into my ear. "You were robbed, boy. I would've given you first prize." Henry pumped my hand up and down till I felt like it would fall off. I knew I should feel grateful for the compliments but all I wanted to do was go home.

I noticed Victoria got her share of handshaking too. Becky hugged her and stood close by while their sleepover friends crowded around with congratulations.

Ms Mitrovika said to Victoria's parents, "You must be so proud of her."

"She could do better if she worked harder," her dad replied.

As Victoria packed up the tablet accessories, her mom said, "That wasn't bad, darling. But you should've listened to me and had more pictures of yourself at the food bank."

Her dad pointed at the game controller. "You know how we feel about those things, Victoria," he said. "It's not coming in the house."

Victoria's lips tightened. Becky patted her shoulder, but Victoria moved away to finish collecting her things.

Then it was all over. We scattered out into the parking lot, and I was left with my parents, Mr. Whitaker, Parker and Sam and their parents. As we walked to our cars, Dad put his arm around me and gave me a squeeze. "That was a tremendous performance," he said. He turned to Mom. "Gracie, don't you think Jelly's as good as me at throwing his voice?"

"Beyond question," she replied. "And I think Jelly's even funnier." She smiled at me as Dad tried to look offended. Mr. and Mrs. Brown laughed.

Victoria and her parents drove by. She stared out the window at me with my family and friends, but she didn't sneer or scowl. She looked kind of sad . . . and wishful.

After the speech competition, life returned to normal. Victoria's win was the talk of the school, and she went back to not noticing me. I could play Rebel Ruckus again with my friends. Parker and I decided to ignore Spencer when he was being a pest. That took the joy out of it for Spencer and he stopped bothering us so much. I have to admit, it was better fun to have more game-playing and less fighting.

On Saturdays, I still went to the food bank with Sam. When Parker didn't have hockey, he and Elsa came with us. Victoria didn't show up there again. Henry was proud of himself. His presentation to the board of directors had gone so well, he'd done extra sales talks and convinced more businesses to partner with the food bank. He'd also aced his first test at night school, and I was giving him computer lessons on Wednesday afternoons.

I saw Kayla and her little sister Addie at the food bank one more time. Kayla said, "My mom says we won't be coming back here 'cause Dad has a new job. I'll miss Bear. But I'll still see you at school — right, Jelly-Joe?"

"Sure, I'll see you on the playground," I said.

Bear put on his squeaky voice and said, "Bye, Addie." He rubbed noses with her and she laughed. Addie gave me a hug and a picture she drew of herself, Bear, Kayla and me holding hands in a garden of flowers. I put it on the wall in my room, next to my Ninja Turtle drawings.

* * * * *

I won't lie; it was a ginormous letdown that I didn't win the speech competition. I really wanted that tablet. But, what I wanted most of all was to beat Victoria. So I didn't exactly get what I wanted. But neither did she.

Even though Victoria won the contest, she wasn't happy. The principal made her carry out her promise to do that big food drive. Oh, that was a good day. Mrs. Muddgrove came to our classroom and said, "I've been impressed by the talent and caring shown by the students of this school." She planted her eyes on Victoria. "In addition to everything she's involved with," Mrs. Muddgrove said, "Victoria offered to organize a food drive for Food Share. It's with pleasure I give her the staff's full support."

We all clapped and cheered while Victoria tried to look pleased. But I could tell she wasn't excited about having to do something so ordinary and close to home. Sam, Parker, Elsa and I signed up for that project. We'll see that Victoria does more than just boss people around. And we'll make sure she doesn't take the credit for everything.

* * * * *

It was two weeks after the competition that it happened. My class had just walked into the computer lab when the announcement came. The secretary's voice droned over the PA system, "Attention all students and teachers. There will be an assembly for the entire school, immediately. Please make your way to the gym."

We looked at Mr. Chan, puzzled. Last week, we'd had an assembly where Victoria, Trina and I went onstage and showed off our medals. Why would there be another one so soon? But Mr. Chan shooed at us with his hands until we lined up at the door.

In the gym, I scooted over to where Parker sat on the floor and waved back to some of the other kids. Roger had made me even more popular than my first speech had. I settled down on the familiar painted floor. It was as cold and hard as ever. But today I didn't mind that, or the crush of shoulders and legs around me. Instead of feeling squished and claustrophobic, it felt warm and cozy to be sitting among friends.

The principal made her way across the stage, holding up her hand and glowering at us all. Her expression didn't scare me anymore. I knew that when stuff mattered, Mrs. Muddgrove was fair and kind. Gradually the noise in the gym died down.

"Students," she said, "I'd like to introduce Mr. Flint."

She gestured to her left, and a man wearing a suit stepped beside her. I hadn't noticed him standing off to the side.

"Mr. Flint," Mrs. Muddgrove continued, "is a representative from the Ministry of Education."

That sounded important. Maybe he'd come to thank us for our fundraising efforts — or congratulate us on the recycling program. Mr. Flint took Mrs. Muddgrove's place at the lectern. He looked like his name. His face was sharp and his grey hair matched his grey suit. Even his voice sounded gravelly when he spoke. "Each year, the ministry issues a request for student artwork to be used in brochures and newsletters. This year, there was a challenge to come up with an image and slogan to address bullying."

Bullying, again? This was getting tedious. With all the presentations and class circles, I'm sure the bullies had learned more about how to bully than they'd ever be able to use in a lifetime.

And this guy needed some help with his speech. Topic: boring. Presentation skills: lacking. Humour: zero.

"We received hundreds of entries and were impressed by their high quality," said Mr. Flint in his monotone. "However, there is someone in this school who captured, with art and words, the very essence of what we all need to do to help stop bullying. I'm here to congratulate and present that student with this certificate."

Everyone in the gym looked around. I saw Becky give Victoria a little poke and mouth, "Was it you?" Victoria shook her head.

Mr. Flint waited for quiet. Then he gestured at the back, and the lights dimmed. The winning poster appeared on the white wall behind the stage.

It was three metres tall and brilliantly lit. A picture of a big kid pushing some little kid around while a bunch of other people stood by and watched. It was in living 3-D coloured pencil.

I knew what the slogan was before I read it: *Speak Up, Speak Out.*

I had written it myself and filled in each of the letters a different colour, with shading and everything. Horrified, I scrutinized the picture of the bully. Yup, there she was, in all her curly-haired glory. Big and mean, my portrait of

Victoria glared out of the picture at everyone in the gym. The look on her real face perfectly matched the expression in my poster.

Mr. Flint said, "The artist will have the satisfaction of knowing his work will be used in the ministry's brochures and displayed in all the schools in the province."

So much for staying under Victoria's radar and making it to middle school alive.

"The winner of this year's art contest is Joseph Miles."

There was no time to feel anything. Parker slapped me on the back till I thought my shoulder blades would cave in, then he pushed me out into the aisle. I wobbled between the seated students and climbed to where Mr. Flint stood waiting to shake my hand. He handed me a piece of paper and an envelope. I turned to go, but Mrs. Muddgrove barred my way and pointed at the microphone. I stepped up to it and, my throat as dry as chalk dust, squawked, "Thank you, Mr. Flint."

The students applauded as I made my way back to my spot on the floor.

"Groovy!" said Parker. "What's in there?"

The envelope in my hand had my name on it but I didn't open it then. Maybe I wanted to stretch out the anticipation. Maybe I didn't want everyone at school to see me look disappointed. Anyway, I put it in my backpack and took it home.

* * * * *

At dinner, I told my mom and dad about winning the poster contest.

"My goodness, Jelly bean," said Mom, "you're just full of surprises this year."

"This is the kind of surprise I like," said Dad.

I showed them the certificate, and then I remembered the envelope. By then I'd convinced myself it held a gift card to some bookstore.

There was a letter inside congratulating me. It mentioned a "scholarship" provided by the Ministry of Education. There was something else inside the envelope — a cheque signed by the Treasurer of Ontario — for two hundred dollars.

It wasn't enough to buy a tablet computer complete with accessories, but it was big enough to do *something*.

Mom said, "Oh my, that's a lot of money."

Dad said, "Way to go, Jelly!"

I wished I'd opened it up in school. Right when Victoria was walking by.

* * * * *

The next day, Parker and Elsa, Sam and I sat on the raised roots of the big tree at the back of the playground, our feet on the soft ground. I looked at the red-brown brick building in the distance. From far away, school seemed even tinier than it felt on the inside. But, although a few weeks ago my life had seemed small and constricted, today it felt like it stretched forever.

"What will you do with all your loot?" asked Parker.

"I don't know," I sighed. "It's such a chore deciding how to spend my fortune. Maybe I'll buy us a new game for your game system."

"But Rebel Ruckus is the best."

So true.

"Y'know," I thought out loud, "I think there might be some people who could use a donation toward a new fridge unit."

Sam grinned and nodded her head enthusiastically.

"I suppose that since you're my best friend," said Parker, "good ideas are bound to rub off on you every once in a while."

I saw, from the corner of my eye, Victoria and Becky strolling in our direction. They stopped a little distance away and Victoria said, loudly, "There's that loser Jelly-fish and his fishy friends." They giggled and turned away.

Parker opened his mouth to yell something but Elsa touched his hand and shook her head.

Sam turned and smiled at me. "You look like a winner to me," she said. Then she turned bright pink.

I didn't know what to do, so I patted her awkwardly on the shoulder and said, "Me too . . . I mean, you too."

Parker bent over and made gagging sounds.

Sam put her arm around me.

There were times when I couldn't think of anything to say. And sometimes I'd been too scared to open my mouth. But this moment was perfect. No words were needed.

That left me speechless.

Acknowledgements

The completion of this book was hugely dependent on moral support. A giant smooch and thank you to Craig Gardner for his tech savvy and for always thinking of me. To Milka Lukic and Theresa Foreshew, I am "greatful" for the coffee and for asking if I've finished the book yet. I've been lucky to belong to writing groups that find the delicate balance between supplying moral support and applying a kick to the pants. Thanks for your brilliance Ann Strickland-Clark, Judi Morris, Julie Whitley, Toni Primavera, Barbara Wood, Donna Kirk, Jan Collis, Karen Kachra, Kimberly Scutt, Linda Shales, Liz Bryant, Sheila Gale, Ruth Edgett and Susan Calvert-Gordon. Enormous gratitude goes to Vicki Daly, David Giannotti and Daniel Giannotti, whose initial readings and comments were invaluable. I'm indebted to Richard Ungar for his optimism and generous critique of the manuscript. Thanks to Brian Henry, the best writing instructor ever, and my colleagues from his classes (especially Irving Ellman, Karin Weber and Sue Shipley) for their inspiration and encouragement. A big thank you to the lovely Sherry Isaac for reminding me that the answers to big questions are usually right under our noses. Thanks to Paul Tammeorg, manager of Partnership West Food Bank, and Brenda Thompson, for making me welcome, showing me around and answering all my questions. Enormous appreciation goes to Aldo Fierro of Scholastic, whose cover design captures the spirit of the story perfectly. I am especially grateful to Anne Shone at Scholastic, whose wisdom and kindness while editing are exceeded only by her good looks and charm (and in case you haven't met her, she's got loads of those).

Praise for Speechless

"Jennifer Mook-Sang brings both comedy and insight to that watershed of middle school: the speech contest . . . A funny, engaging read that proves that even our deepest fears can be hilarious."

—National Reading Campaign

"*Speechless* was so funny that it reminded me of . . . 1970's Judy Blume . . . Highly recommended."

—CM: *Canadian Review of Materials*

Awards & Honours

★Shortlisted, Red Cedar Book Awards (British Columbia Young Readers' Choice), 2017

★Shortlisted, MYRCA (Manitoba Young Readers' Choice Award), 2017

★Shortlisted, Surrey Schools' Book of the Year, 2017

★Shortlisted, Ontario Library Association Silver Birch Award for Fiction, 2016

★Shortlisted, IODE Violet Downey Book Award, 2016

★Shortlisted, Diamond Willow Award (Saskatchewan Young Readers' Choice), 2016

★Ontario Library Association Best Bet, 2015

★CBC (Canadian Broadcasting Corporation) Best Books of 2015

Visit www.scholastic.ca/speechless for more *Speechless* fun!